EMPULSE

DEBORAH D. MOORE

A PERMUTED PRESS BOOK

ISBN: 978-1-68261-200-2
ISBN (eBook): 978-1-68261-201-9

EMPulse
© 2017 by Deborah D. Moore
All Rights Reserved

Cover art by Christian Bentulan

PERMUTED
PRESS

Permuted Press, LLC
permutedpress.com

To Preppers everywhere

Is it that you think of me so little,
Or that you think so little of me?

–D.D. Moore

ACKNOWLEDGEMENTS

Sometimes it's easy to say thank you and sometimes not. I wrote this book with very few knowing what I was doing and how it was progressing until I was done. My two beta readers, Sherry F. and Tom M. were stunned that I was done so quickly, and that they had so little to suggest, but what they did helped a great deal. They were both delighted I tried something new.

I could never have gotten this far without the encouragement of my family: my sons Eric and Jason, my siblings Tom, Pam, and Jan, and my friends who listened to me babble on and on about plot lines. So thank you. Also to my internet friends who unknowingly added fodder to the story when I asked innocent questions about EMPs.

The final, warmest thank you goes to my editor Felicia A. Sullivan for tweaking the manuscript, and to Michael Wilson at Permuted Press for his faith in me, and to the awesome staff at Permuted Press for all their hard work and diligence to make my books the best they can be. In a world where visual effects are what captures the attention, the Permuted Press art department that develops the covers—totally rock!

CHAPTER ONE

"Kyle, listen to me," Adele Michaels said to her ex-husband through the plate glass window. "I'm not going to put up bail for you again. Last time was the last time, I told you that! Plus, this is not a place you can get bailed out of anyway."

If it were, his corporate lawyers would have him out already. What he really needed her to do was drop the charges. Her acute peripheral vision took in the institutional pale green walls and bolted-down furniture. Those vivid blue eyes didn't miss anything.

"But, babe, you can't leave me in here," Kyle Polez pleaded.

"Yes I can, Kyle," she said calmly. "Besides, you need the full course of the anger management program that's available here."

That program involved drugs, and for all his faults Kyle was very anti-drug use of any nature, even helpful ones. He did not believe he was bi-polar, or psychotic or violent, he only "got a little upset occasionally." Therefore, he didn't need any personality changing drugs.

Yeah, right.

His nostrils flared, and the anger flashed through his pale blue eyes and was gone just as quickly. He ran his fingers through the buzz-cut hairstyle forced on him. "If I finish that program, will you take me back?" he asked hopefully, knowing what her answer was already.

"No, Kyle, I will not. We've been divorced for six months and I will not go through that again," Adele stated emphatically.

"I don't recognize that divorce. You are still my wife!" he screamed at her, pounding his fist on the chipped and scarred Formica table. The guard at the door took a step forward.

"I'm leaving now, and I'm not coming back. Is there anything you need that they will let you have?"

He gave her a forced sweet smile. "Gum." She reached into her shoulder bag that she was also using as a sling, brought out a large pack of Juicy Fruit, Kyle's favorite, and handed it to the guard.

Adele held her head high as she walked from the mental hospital to her car through the oppressive October heat of West Texas, her high heels clicking on the pavement. Once inside the tinted windows of her powder blue Lexus, she slouched and rested her damp forehead against the leather steering wheel while the air conditioning pumped the cool air into her face.

Her fractured arm ached from the makeshift sling and she rested it on her lap. There was no way she was going to let that violent and vile man see her in the pain he'd caused.

They'd had a fairytale wedding. Kyle Polez, millionaire many times over, had rented an entire castle in Switzerland. The guests were treated to every extravagance possible for an entire week, and Kyle showered Adele with unforgettable and expensive gifts. It was a magical time.

It hadn't even been a month after their wedding, and he was smacking her around. Then it was his fists. The last time he pushed her down the stairs. That was when she filed for an annulment. Kyle fought that, and she filed for a divorce. He fought that too, only she won because she didn't want anything from him, not a dime. Anthony Evers, Adele's high-priced lawyer, pushed her to take the million dollars Kyle offered. She did, under duress, and it still sat in the bank, untouched. She didn't want it and didn't need it. The name Adele Michaels was well known and her art kept her very comfortable. No, she didn't want his money, and she certainly didn't want *him*.

After reviewing her doctor's records, her lawyer also advised Adele to get a restraining order on Kyle, which she did. It enraged him even more. He stalked her to the point she was afraid to leave her penthouse apartment. When he caught her waiting at the curb for a taxi, he tried pulling her into his car, twisting her arm to the point of breaking it. The intervention of the hotel security saved her, and put Kyle in jail. He was soon transferred to the posh mental hospital.

Adele put the sleek car in gear. It was one of those expensive gifts Kyle had given her the week of their wedding. She was going to miss the smooth, quiet ride. She also knew Kyle had a tracking device installed in it, someplace her mechanic couldn't find.

With the title in hand, she left the car at the Lexus dealer on consignment and took a taxi to the Chevy dealer to pick up her new Tahoe.

"This is a real beauty, Miss Michaels," the salesman said, handing her the keys, delighted that she was writing a check, no financing, no hassles, no questions.

Adele walked around the deep maroon vehicle, studying the lines. "I'm assuming for the price it has all the bells and whistles?"

"Yes, ma'am! Built in Wi-Fi; touch start, programmed to your fingerprint; computer screens on the backs of the front seats; back-up camera; automatic fold-down rear seats for extra storage space; foot activated rear hatch. It also has the larger engine you requested and the extra gas tank," he assured her.

"Four wheel drive, right?"

"All wheel on demand, yes."

"Great." Adele handed him the cashier's check. "I do appreciate how quickly my requests were dealt with, Mr. Jones." She handed him several folded bills, five one-hundred dollar bills to be exact. "I was never here." He smiled and nodded, putting the bills in his pocket without looking.

Adele drove out of the parking lot and headed toward the storage locker she had rented where most of her things were. All she was interested in were her painting supplies and some of her clothes. All of her beautiful gowns and expensive shoes she left behind. She wouldn't need them where she was going. Her fine jewelry was locked away in a safe in her attorney's office, with the exception of a few pieces she'd bought herself. The ring Kyle had given her, twenty-one perfect marquis-cut diamonds set in platinum, had been returned to him through their lawyers. She hated the gaudy ring and would have preferred a simple gold band. Her fingers were now bare.

CHAPTER TWO

Adele drove for hours, stopping only to gas up and to use a restroom. She wanted to put as much distance between her and Kyle as possible. Kyle was not only insanely jealous, but insane, and he scared the hell out of her. She was hoping that the months he would spend in that institution, with its keyless locks and fenced in manicured grounds, would dim his obsession of her and she would be free of him.

Until that happened, Adele was going into hiding. No one, not even her own mother knew where she would be.

Nestled in the Rocky Mountains, the Geo Dome Resort was a series of monolithic domes partially buried in the rocky soil, and claimed to have lots of privacy with limited amenities. There was the usual skiing and snowshoeing in the winter, and hiking, mountain biking, fishing, and horseback riding in the warmer months, plus a restaurant and lounge was available, mostly for the weekend guests. Adele wasn't a weekend guest; she had leased one of the more secluded domes for a year: A year to heal her broken arm and her broken spirit. The arm was nearly there; her spirit would take longer.

Adele pulled into the parking lot of a bulk food store in Butte, Montana. There were no quick-marts where she was going. In fact, there were barely any roads. She needed food and supplies for at least six months of seclusion. In the spring, she could come back and restock.

She filled the back of the Tahoe with boxes stacked to the ceiling: Boxes filled with pasta and rice; dried herbs and spices; canned fish and meat; juice and sauces and soups; cases of wine and good liquor. Adele filled coolers with fine cheeses, fresh meat, and poultry. Another box of condiments, olives for her martinis and pickled asparagus for the occasional bloody Mary. There was no reason to not indulge her expensive tastes. The boxes nearly obscured her rear view and she was thankful for that backing-up camera.

Before leaving Texas, Adele had made lists and more lists of things she would need. Things she remembered her mother always having on hand. Her mother was a prepper, and was often scorned for her way of life, but Adele fondly remembered that they never ran out of anything during those long, snowy months in northern Michigan.

"Can you tell me how to get to Johnson Lane?" Adele asked the clerk at the Taylor Mayde gas station, paying cash for her fill up. "For some reason my GPS can't find it."

"Oh, that's because it was renamed a few months back. It used to be Hog Back Road," the young girl answered. "Not much up that way. Where ya going?"

"I'll try that, thanks," Adele replied, avoiding the girl's question. As far as she was concerned, it was nobody's business where she was headed.

She entered the old name and the GPS immediately found the route. Breathing a sigh of relief, she put the car in gear and left.

The Geo Dome Resort was even more impressive than the website pictures. Built into the side of a mountain, there were at least a dozen domes of varying sizes, some clustered and some separate. Adele pulled into the parking area of a small dome that was placed at the front, presumably the office. Behind it was another larger dome that appeared to be attached to the office. Adele found the concept intriguing.

"Welcome, Miss Michaels," the young man behind the counter greeted her. "Your dome is on the outer perimeter, as you requested. It has a private parking area as well. The boxes you shipped are already inside," he said, handing her a set of keys and a large packet of information.

She silently studied him: close to her age of thirty-eight, maybe a little younger; perhaps six foot tall; muscular like he worked out regularly; hazel eyes; and collar length sandy brown hair. Nice looking, too. Her artist's eye took in the details quickly. She glanced at his name tag, which read: Jeffery Atkins, General Manager.

"Keys?" she asked, amused.

"Yes. Here we make our own power, which is a lot more reliable than the grid. That being said, we still can go down on occasion. Keys assure you can always get in your unit. Keycards could get tricky." He smiled warmly at her. "Do you need any assistance with your luggage?" His eyes wanted to roam her lithe body. He willed them to stay fixed on her face, which wasn't that hard; it was a beautiful face: deep blue eyes, short blonde hair, high cheekbones.

"As a matter of fact—" She was interrupted when a young teen ran up to the counter.

"Hey, Jeff, you got anything I can do for a few bucks? Mom won't give me any more money for the game room. I know we're leaving tomorrow, but I'm bored out of my skull." The boy leaned on the desk, oblivious to Adele.

Adele immediately took advantage of the intrusion, and the fact that the boy was leaving soon made it perfect. "Say, how would you like twenty dollars for helping me unload my car?"

"Awesome, lady, thanks!"

Adele glanced at the general manager, who gave a slight nod, letting her know the kid was okay.

"That's a lot of boxes," Tony said, staring in the back of the Tahoe.

"That's why I need help," she said pleasantly. "Don't worry, I'll make it worth your time. All you need to do is get them in kitchen; I'll do the rest."

Adele carried her suitcase in and set it in the private bedroom, admiring the simple lines and the soft colors of the condo unit. Tony set two boxes in the kitchen and went back for more. It took her three trips to bring in her art supplies and the rest of her personal items.

Seeing the boy struggle with one of the coolers, she grabbed one of the handles and helped him. Together they unloaded the SUV of everything.

"Is there something wrong with your arm, ma'am?" Tony asked tentatively.

"Yes, Tony, it was broken a few months ago and is still kind of sore, which is the reason I needed help," Adele told the boy.

"Is there anything else I can help you with?" Tony asked sheepishly.

"I think I can handle things from here on, but thank you for asking." She got her wallet and took out two twenties. "I really appreciate the help. Go have some fun." His eyes glowed at the extra twenty and he ran out.

With the boy gone, Adele looked at the stacks and stacks of boxes, thankful no one else would know how much she had unloaded. Not that it mattered; it was that she was a private person and didn't like answering questions. Questions led to more questions, like why she didn't want to go out to eat, why was she hiding, and who was she hiding *from*? No, questions were not good because the answers led back to Kyle, and the name "Kyle Polez" was extremely well known in the computer world.

She dragged the two heavy coolers over to the side-by-side refrigerator. The meat and chicken had already been packaged for the freezer so it was quick to fill that side, leaving out one steak for her dinner later. Her cheeses took an entire shelf in the refrigerator and she found spaces for her fruit, eggs, fresh vegetables, and lettuces.

Her arm began to ache from the activity, which told her it was time to take a break. She put her laptop on the desk next to the front door and plugged everything in. While the computer booted up and charged, Adele wandered around the dome. It was roomy, though not huge. At least it was furnished. A large flat-screen TV, sectional couch, reading lamp, coffee table arranged to effectively divide the room in half, and a small dining table off to the side. It was sparse but comfortable and spoke of efficiency. The woodstove in the corner was a model with glass doors to view the fire; much more practical than a fireplace, she thought. There wasn't any furniture blocking the large picture window, which was good, since that's where her art table needed to go.

The bedroom was a separate, smaller dome, attached like the check-in office to whatever was behind it. It was adequate, with a queen sized bed, a dresser done in polished oak and walnut, a walk-in closet with sliding mirrored doors and an attached bath with a garden spa tub, and laundry. She hung a few things in the closet and the rest went into the dresser. She also carefully put her 9mm handgun in the nightstand, close to the bed. Her toiletries she set on the marble sink in the bathroom. She smiled with approval at the garden tub and separate shower stall. Towels and linens were also furnished; not what she was accustomed to but they would do until she could replace them. She fully intended to replace them if she was going to stay as long as she planned. For the last several years, Adele had lived a life of luxury, one she had earned through hard work, and it had been easy to get accustomed to it. She saw no reason not to indulge herself now that she could afford it.

The kitchen was sectioned from the other space by a work island done in the same soft green ceramic tile that graced the counters under the numerous cabinets. Against the work island and slightly elevated was an eating bar with four padded oak stools. The dome was one very large room. That solitary picture window had a magnificent view that took in the mountain and woods and the other domes.

Adele opened one of the cases of wine and extracted a bottle of red.

"Damn, I hope there's a cork opener in this place," she muttered, rummaging through the drawers. She sighed in relief finding what she needed.

Taking her glass, Adele walked the perimeter of the dome taking in the panoramic view. There was also a sliding glass door that led to the private patio where a gas grill sat. She opened the door and stepped out, then quickly retreated when she felt the chilled late-October air coming down from the Rocky Mountains.

"I think I'm going to need different clothes!" She shivered and jotted something down on a notepad by the humming computer. She dumped out the packet given to her and found the Wi-Fi access codes and typed them in. Only thing of interest in her email was the deadline schedule from her agent and the gallery she usually dealt with.

Adele Michaels painted and was in high demand. She did large watercolors to get the detail she desired. It was then printed in smaller, frame-able versions that would be numbered and signed. The prints brought a good price, while the originals went for thousands. Well, those she sold. Most of them she kept. Once all the prints were sold, the artwork was then transferred to greeting cards and stationery, and that was where the real money was. Thousands and thousands of boxes of her cards were sold every year. Her royalties on the Christmas cards last year alone paid for the new Tahoe. She had a year to come up with a dozen new designs and this might be the perfect place to do it, she thought, staring at the impressive mountains.

Adele stacked the four empty boxes by the door. Putting away the canned goods was exhausting, especially after driving all day. She decided to do the rest tomorrow. Right now, that garden tub called to her.

She turned the water on hot and waited until the water was over the jets before testing them. The water swirled and bubbled, just like it should. She knew to not use bubble bath. That happened only once, and Kyle had beaten her for the mess it made. Adele added a few drops of scented oil, and dropped her clothes on the floor, sliding into the pulsating water. She sighed contentedly and took a sip of her wine.

CHAPTER THREE

Adele sat on the floor, the parts to her art table spread around her. She sighed and picked up the directions again. Things finally started to make sense and within a half hour the table was assembled. The other boxes that had been pre-shipped contained a rainbow of new watercolor inks, her preferred medium, plus over two hundred sheets of specialized watercolor paper. In the supplies she carried with her to the dome were her brushes, and there were over a hundred of those. Some were large, wide and flat for moistening the paper; some had only a dozen fine sable hairs to create minute detail. Every one of them had a purpose and every one of them she used.

Adele lined up a series of cups on the art table and sorted the brushes, handle down. Not only could she then see which brush was which, but it also protected the bristles that way. The inks were sorted by color and placed in trays for easy access. Often she would use only four or five colors, and those would stay on the table until she was finished with that piece of work. On occasion, she used only one color and those were the most dramatic, and the most sought after.

She stretched her back, poured another cup of coffee, and frowned. She had forgotten to pick up her favorite coffee creamer. She added that to her growing list. She had been there for only five days, and already needed to go for more supplies. After looking through the refrigerator one last time and adding butter to her list, she grabbed her keys and purse, heading for her car and that small town at the other end of the road.

Adele liked to think of herself as adventuresome, though it was limited to knowing where she was or how to get to where she had been. With that in mind, she drove her new Tahoe around the small town of Avon, trying to familiarize herself with it.

The map on her computer screen that was built into the dashboard said the town had only fifteen hundred year-round residents. A far cry from the cities of Dallas and Houston she had once lived in, and Abilene, the city she'd fled from, leaving Kyle.

On one of the main streets, she spotted the Wilderness Outfitters store that had an ad on the back of the brochure from the resort. Adele was hoping it could outfit her in some new and warmer clothes.

She browsed the aisles, selecting flannel shirts in her size, and dropped an armload on the front desk. She went back for packages of silk long-johns, heavy socks, and sweaters. Adding a couple pairs of flannel lined jeans and fleece loungers, Adele thought she might be close to being done until she spotted the shoe section.

"I need to take these socks out of the package to try on with boots," she said to the sales clerk, ripping open the package.

"Sure thing," the young woman said, shocked at the pile of clothing that was still growing. She spoke softly into the microphone on her lapel, "Henry, I need some assistance on the front counter please."

Adele sat in a chair with several pairs of boots on the floor around her, and slipped on the heavy socks.

"Can I help you find something?" an older gentleman asked.

She looked up and smiled. "Yes, I need these in a half size larger." Adele handed him the boots she had rejected. "I didn't realize the socks would make such a difference." He returned with the proper size and she slipped her foot in comfortably and stood. "Yes, these are good. Thank you."

"From the pile on the counter, you could make our monthly sales quota in one hour," Henry chuckled, taking the boxes from her.

"I was unprepared, clothing-wise," Adele admitted.

"How long will you be staying in the area? Perhaps I can make a few suggestions," he offered.

"All winter."

"You'll need better boots than what you've selected. What about outerwear?" he prodded. "Like a jacket, hats, gloves?"

"Oh, I forgot about those! Lead me!"

They moved to the other end of the store, where Adele selected one short jacket and a knee-length down coat in dove gray, hats and gloves to match. On the way to the checkout, she spotted a display of long skirts and took two.

Passing the weapons counter, she stopped. "Henry, I need a brick of 9mm hollow points. Can you get them for me?" He looked a bit startled but covered it well. He pulled a set of keys out of his pocket and opened the case.

The clerk finished ringing up the items and Adele handed over her platinum debit card. The clerk eyed it and was surprised when the sale went through without a hesitation.

"Ms. Michaels, please allow me to help you take these packages to your car," Henry said. He took as many bags as he could handle and followed her out the door to the Tahoe, going back once for another load. As Adele had spent nearly three thousand dollars on good, top of the line clothing, it was the least he could do.

Adele had always loved to shop and now that she could afford it, she insisted on quality.

The next and final stop was the Walstroms super store where she replenished what fresh foods she had eaten over the last week, and stocked up on coffee creamer, butter, softer tissue paper, and a better quality cork opener. She decided she might have to go back to Butte for the Egyptian cotton sheets she loved and thicker bath towels. That would have to wait though. She was tired. She realized she had forgotten to take something from the freezer for dinner, and grabbed several frozen pizzas. A pizza was comfort food when she forgot about eating for hours on end.

As part of the security for the resort, observation cameras were mounted strategically, and discreetly, around the compound. Jeff Atkins hit a few keys on his computer and zoomed in on Adele's location, watching her make several trips to empty her car. He thought for a few minutes while he watched, and then exited that program and ran a search on her name.

"I knew that name was familiar!" he whispered to himself. Her website offered a view into the gallery of all her paintings. "Wow."

CHAPTER FOUR

Adele finished hanging her new clothes in the large closet. She had a pile of items that would touch her skin, like the socks and long-johns, that would need to be washed first. Hiking boots, snow boots, and casual boots, now free from their boxes and tissue paper, sat on the floor of the closet, beside her warm, furry slippers.

She closed her eyes, rubbing them slightly, then ran her fingers through her short blonde hair and sighed. Short hair was new to her. She had always worn it long until the day Kyle knocked her unconscious and hacked it all off. Her stylist actually wept when he saw the hatchet job. An hour later, Adele had a smart new cut.

A quick glance at her watch told her it was after six in the evening. In the kitchen she set the oven to preheat and pulled out one of the pizzas.

She dragged one of the tall stools over to her art table to stare out the window at the sun setting behind the mountain. It would make a good painting. She captured the scene and the array of colors with her camera.

All the activity for the day, plus pizza and wine for dinner while watching the evening news, was enough to put Adele into a deep, dreamless sleep.

With the coffee almost ready in her French press, Adele stretched and touched her toes, loosening up her back. She spread out the papers from the check-in packet and found a resort map. Hiking trails were clearly marked, as were the bike and horse trails; none of them were the same. She didn't care about the cross country trails since she didn't ski, however the snowshoe trail might give her something to do one afternoon once there was snow.

She took her fresh cup of coffee over to the computer as her new cellphone rang. A surge of panic rose in her throat until she remembered she gave the number only to her mother and her lawyer.

"Hi, Mom!" Adele said, mustering as much enthusiasm as she could. "You're up early."

"I'm always up early," Alden Michaels replied. "So where are you and how are you doing?" she said, getting right to the point.

"I'm in Montana at a resort in the Rocky Mountains, and so far I'm doing fine," she answered, knowing her mother always had her best interests at heart. "I've been here a week and I think I'm about settled in."

"Have you done any painting yet?"

"Not yet, I've been busy stocking up on supplies," Adele replied. "I'm going to take a walk this morning and pick up some local leaves and such to use in my first painting."

Paintings by Adele Michaels always had bits and pieces imbedded somewhere on the canvas; sometimes they were even prominent or the main focus.

"Stocking up, eh? What do you have?"

"The usual, Mom. Lots of soups, pasta, rice, all those things you taught me to keep on hand."

"How much do you have in the freezer?" Alden asked with a *tsk* in her voice.

"The freezer is full, and so is the refrigerator. Don't be such a worry wart!"

"Sorry, dear, I still worry about you."

"I appreciate that, Mom, really." Knowing her mother wouldn't be happy until she could remind Adele about something she forgot, she asked, "Is there anything I should add?"

Alden perked right up. "What kind of stove do you have? Gas or electric?"

"The entire condo is electric, why?"

"It's winter, Adele, and you're in the mountains. What if you lose power? How are you going to warm that soup? What about lights and heat?"

Adele thought for a moment. Her mother was right. That *was* something she hadn't thought about. "There's a small town nearby with a super Walstroms. What should I pick up?"

"Oh, Adele, I taught you better than that! Okay, in the camping section find a two burner camp stove, preferably kerosene but propane will do. Are you writing this down?" Without waiting for an answer, she kept going. "One good lantern that you can carry outside, at least two oil lamps, and don't forget the fuel for all of it. You might want a battery lamp too. That will give you light without additional heat. In fact, get two or three of those, and don't forget a good supply of batteries."

"My mom the prepper. What would I do without you?" Adele laughed. She wrote all that down, starting a new shopping list, and added some candles. Those would be nice around the bathtub some night. Maybe she would go to Butte sooner than expected.

"Um, Adele, how is Kyle and where is he?" Alden asked carefully.

"Mom, I don't care *how* he is, I only care *where* he is, and that's locked away in a mental hospital. He's not my husband anymore and not my responsibility! Just drop it, okay?" Adele knew that came out harsh. "I'm sorry, Mom, I don't want to talk about him."

"Yes, dear, but promise me you will pick up the stove and lamps soon. Remember, you can't prepare tomorrow for what happens today!"

CHAPTER FIVE

"Good morning, Miss Michaels," Jeff said pleasantly. "Are you enjoying your stay with us?"

"So far everything is fine, Mr. Atkins," Adele answered. "I have a couple of questions though."

"I will certainly do my best to answer them, if…" he smiled gently, "you call me Jeff."

"Since I will be around for a while, I can do that, provided you call me Adele." She returned his smile.

"Now that we have that settled, what can I do for you?"

"First, what is the building behind here? The one that looks attached."

"That's the restaurant, and beside it is the rec and game room. Would you like a tour?" he offered.

"Maybe some other time. Right now I'm looking forward to a walk, which brings up my next question. Where do the trails start and are they well marked? I wouldn't want to get lost!"

"All the trails are well marked, although on occasion signs do come down from the weather. We try our best to keep them up. And you're in luck! In about a half hour I'm expecting a school bus of sixth graders and their teachers for a nature walk. Would you care to join me? There is little for me to do except to keep them on the trails; the teachers will do the rest."

"I would love to. Thank you. I need to get my camera, so don't leave without me!" She hurried up the hill to her condo. She put her digital camera and a collection box in a backpack along with two bottles of water, and was back in the parking lot as the bus pulled in.

The day was a moderate seventy degrees, with clear blue skies and bright sunshine. Adele took a deep breath of the clean mountain air and smiled.

"Smells good doesn't it?" Jeff said into her ear, noting that she didn't wear any perfume.

"Oh, yes, reminds me of Michigan." She turned toward him as they continued walking, crunching on the fallen autumn leaves. "The children are very well behaved." The class of fourteen students and three teachers were ahead of them on the well marked trail. Occasionally the adults stopped the kids and pointed out an interesting fall growth or tracks in the dirt, and Jeff always lingered behind making sure everyone stayed with the group.

"Yes, they are, and that's why they are always welcomed back, although there have been an occasion or two when boys being boys, had to be disciplined." Jeff took her arm when she stumbled on a tree root, then removed it quickly. As attractive as he found her, getting too familiar with the guests was a bad idea.

Adele took several pictures of the wildlife they spotted, but mostly of the trees and low growth, also taking samples that she could add to a painting. A short time later, they were back in the parking lot.

"Are all the trails that short of a walk?" she asked Jeff.

"No, there are some longer ones," he replied. "I try not to keep the kids out more than an hour though. They get bored easy."

"An hour? It felt much shorter than that." Adele watched the kids scramble into the bus and wave goodbye.

"How about that tour now? It won't take long, I promise, and you should get to know your way around here and what we have to offer," Jeff said.

The game room was the first area they passed. Apparently it needed, and got, more supervision when the resort was busy. "Youngsters like Tony are right at home here and would spend all their time playing the games instead of enjoying the outdoors like their parents think they should. I've considered closing it." They continued down the wide hallway and he pushed open the double glass doors into the restaurant.

"Impressive," Adele said, taking in the concrete and copper waterfall in the center of the room.

"It helps to add humidity to the air," Jeff explained, "and it's soothing. Here's one of the new menus for you to take back with you. It lists the regular weekly meals like the Friday Fish Fry, although there are daily specials that the chef thinks up, depending on what comes in fresh."

"I tend to eat at home," Adele murmured.

"I've noticed. But there may come a time when you want to get out and enjoy something different, so keep us in mind," he said cheerfully.

Adele was in high spirits after her walk, until she saw her condo door slightly ajar. Cautiously she pushed the door open more and heard water running. She silently stepped inside and quickly looked around. Standing at the sink with her back to Adele, stood a young woman.

"Who are you and what are you doing here?" Adele yelled.

The girl spun around. "Oh, geesh, you scared me!" she said with her wet hand splayed on her chest.

"Who are you?" Adele repeated with a snarl.

"Oh, I'm sorry, ma'am, I'm Beth, the housekeeper. I'm only cleaning up," she replied.

"I didn't ask for a housekeeper!" Adele was thoroughly upset having someone in here when she was gone. She didn't like anyone snooping around.

"I didn't mean to upset you, Miss Michaels. Your condo rent includes weekly housekeeping. I change and wash the sheets and towels, clean up the kitchen, dust, mop, and vacuum, things like that," Beth said. "Didn't Mr. Atkins tell you?"

"No, he didn't." Adele backed off, trying to calm herself. "Is this your regular day?"

"Yes, ma'am, Tuesdays will be your day, unless you wish to change that. We always try to work around the tenants' preferred schedule. Or you can cancel the service completely," Beth said contritely, looking down. "Since there are only six units currently occupied, I work only two or three days a week now. I'm sure looking forward to the holidays when I can get back to work full time." Beth turned back to the sink, shut the water off ,and dried her hands.

The hint wasn't lost on Adele. "You lose pay if I cancel the service?"

"I get paid by the hour, Miss Michaels, and I'm a good worker. But I understand that not everyone wants a maid, even a bonded one like me."

"I see." Adele looked around. The place did look much neater, and she was accustomed to bi-weekly maid service at her penthouse apartment. Not having to hassle with certain chores would give her more time to work, and that Beth was bonded was a plus. "When will you be done here?"

"I'm about finished. I was just washing the coffee pot," Beth said.

"I'll see you next week, then," Adele said, stepping into her bedroom.

Once Beth left, Adele downloaded her camera into the computer and set the samples she'd collected in a tray to air dry. It had been a good day. No, other than the surprise of a housekeeper, it had been a *great* day. It was the first day in a long time that she felt relaxed and hadn't worried about Kyle finding her. In fact, she hadn't thought about Kyle at all.

CHAPTER SIX

Adele put the camp stove, lanterns, packs of batteries, propane bottles, and oil lamps in the back of her huge and mostly empty closet. The candles and matches went into the bottom drawer of the bathroom vanity. Now she could tell her mother she was indeed set for a power outage that would likely never come.

"It's time to get to work, kiddo," she said aloud to herself. She'd done enough stalling and running around. Though honestly, most of what she had left the resort for were items that made her feel comfortable, and safe.

She pushed her art table closer to the big window to take advantage of the early afternoon sunlight. Rusty orange, green, and black ink sat next to the numerous brushes and the four small bowls of plain tap water. She laid a sheet of heavy watercolor paper on the table and brushed it with the tepid water... and she began.

Four hours later Adele stood and stretched her back and her neck. She opened a fresh bottle of wine and after pouring a glass, walked back to her work table.

"Oh, this is looking good," she said aloud. She moved the table so she could walk completely around it and see the new painting from all angles. There were pine needles strategically placed under the wet tissue paper, pine needles from the walk she took with Jeff a few days earlier; there were splashes of orange and of green, watered down and moved around. Adele reached into the box of ink and brought out a dark brown. This, she thought, would make a better accent than the black, but didn't put the black away. Not just yet.

The sun was nearly set. Time to quit and let everything dry. It was a good start. Adele dipped her finger into her wine and dripped some of the ruby liquid onto the paper at a corner, then tipped it so it would run and travel. *Now* it can dry, she thought.

Another sip of wine and her stomach rumbled with hunger. While at Walstroms she had picked up a pre-cooked chicken. All it needed was reheating, and a salad. Always a salad; it was her favorite part of dinner.

She took her dinner to the coffee table and switched on the big TV. She flipped through the channels to find some news. It wasn't good. The powers that be were considering more sanctions on North Korea for arming a missile with a nuclear device and threatening to launch it at the U.S. She wondered how sanctions would stop a nutcase like the leader of North Korea.

Adele woke at eight o'clock, surprised she had slept the entire night without waking. She surmised it was the lower stress level and that she was painting again. Painting always took her away from everything that bothered her. Kyle didn't *allow* her to paint. He said she didn't need the money anymore; she had him. He didn't understand that it was the creativity that compelled her to paint, not the money. On the other hand, maybe he did, and it was one more thing he needed to take away from her so he had control.

With a fresh cup of coffee in hand, she circled the art table, studying what she had done the day before, and she was pleased.

She rinsed her cup out and sat on a stool in front of the new painting. While there was a painting on the table, there was never anything else. Coffee cups and wine glasses, anything that could spill, were forbidden in her mind. Still in a rumpled t-shirt and brightly colored thin flannel lounging pants, she picked up a fine-tipped brush.

The delicate brush strokes that accented and outlined different aspects of the painting were mostly a muted dark brown, and blended softly into the other colors, giving life to the canvas. A touch of watered down black brought a pine needle to the front, giving depth to the others around it. She worked two handed, one with ink, one with water to keep that blending in motion. There were times it took weeks to do one painting; other times only a day or two. This one was almost complete. On the back of the paper, she listed the exact names of the inks used, the title, *Wind Swept,* and she signed it. Once she decided what angle felt right to her, she would add the title to the bottom front and sign it again.

Adele rinsed and washed her brushes, setting them upright to dry after twirling them in the palm of her hand. The wind picked up and tossed snowflakes at the glass window, demanding her attention. At first she thought the weather had dimmed the sun, until she saw the clock read six-thirty p.m. Other than that one cup of coffee, she hadn't drank or eaten all day, and she was still in her pajamas. She believed that finishing a piece needed celebrating. This was no exception. She eyed the laminated menu Jeff insisted she keep.

Adele dressed in one of her new long skirts after she showered, added a touch of makeup, and wrapped in her new long coat, walked down to the resort restaurant.

Jeff Atkins sat at a table along the windows and facing the entrance door of the elegant yet casual restaurant, so he could see who came and went. He was delightfully surprised when Adele walked in. He immediately stood and walked toward her.

"Good evening, Adele," he said. "Are you here for dinner or only drinks? Both are gourmet tonight."

"Dinner is what I had in mind, Jeff, *and* drinks. I'm celebrating," she replied.

"I love celebrations. What's the occasion?" he asked, guiding her to the table he had just vacated.

"I finished a new piece of… work," she said, and automatically sat when he pulled a chair out for her. When he sat too, she noticed his drink and realized he had placed her at *his* table. "I didn't intend to interrupt your evening, Jeff." She started to stand.

"Please sit, Adele. You're not interrupting anything," he reassured her. "In fact you've brightened my evening. What would you like to drink?" he asked as a waiter came up to their table.

"May I see the wine list, please?" She smiled at the young man standing there. He had come prepared and set the wine menu and the food menu down in front of her, then silently stepped back. She quickly glanced at the offerings. "A bottle of this chardonnay," she said, pointing, "and I'll have whatever the chicken special is."

The waiter took the menus and departed.

"A good choice on both accounts," Jeff said. "I already ordered the chicken. You will be pleased with your choice, I hope."

A moment later the waiter returned with two chilled glasses, and opened the likewise chilled bottle in front of her, poured them each a taste, and nestled the bottle in an ice bucket. Jeff raised his glass and touched hers. "Congratulations on finishing your painting."

Adele was startled. "You know I paint?"

Jeff chuckled. "Of course I do, Miss Adele Michaels, renowned artist. And, yes, I know who you are. I'm an admirer of your work."

"I see."

"No one else here and no one on the staff knows. I understand that for some reason you need the seclusion and privacy my resort offers. Your secret is safe with me," he promised.

"I hope, for my sake, I can believe that," she whispered, and tried hard to ignore her mounting anxiety.

"That was truly delightful," Adele said, finishing the last bite of her boneless chicken. "The pesto sauce was light enough to taste the chicken seasonings, yet enough to taste the sauce. At first I thought the angel hair pasta would be too weak for the sauce, but it was perfect. The food here is excellent, I'm surprised you're not busier." She finished off her glass of wine and ordered a spot of port.

"You have excellent taste in wine, Adele," Jeff said. "That chard was perfect for the chicken. As for not being busy, we close the hotel portion for the month of November for deep cleaning and maintenance. The long term units, like yours, stay available, although only four of the six units are occupied right now. Things tend to get a lot busier once it snows." His eyes were drawn to a side window. "Speaking of snow, it looks like the snow predicted for tomorrow has arrived early. Can I drive you back to the condo?" he offered when she had finished her drink.

"I don't melt," she laughed. "I think I'll walk, but thank you."

"Then I will walk with you. These inclines, slight as they are, can get slippery until I can plow and salt."

"There you are, safe and sound," Jeff said when they arrived at her door. She had slipped only once and he'd tucked her arm in his for the rest of the walk.

"Thank you," Adele said, hesitantly. "Would you like to see the new painting?"

"I would be honored!" he beamed. "May I stop by tomorrow though? I really need to attend to these roads."

CHAPTER SEVEN

Adele woke with a slight headache from too little to eat and then too much wine. Deciding a few aspirins would solve that, she headed into the bathroom.

With her cup of coffee she wandered to the picture window and was shocked how much snow had fallen overnight. There had to be a foot out there and she gave an involuntary shudder at how cold it looked. She looked longingly at the woodstove and wondered where the supply of wood was. Today would be a break-day, a day to relax and to clear her head to get ready for the next painting. A fire would be really nice.

Dressed for the blowing snow, Adele opened the front door cautiously, and still got a face full from the blast of arctic air. She closed the door behind her and ventured into the carport. On the wall adjacent to the house hung two pairs of snowshoes, two bicycles, a hatchet, and a shovel. On the opposite side there was a short stack of wood and a leather sling. She put four pieces of wood in the sling, tested its weight, and added two more pieces. After making a nice, neat stack of two dozen pieces next to the stove, it dawned on her there was no kindling.

Adele was nearly done splitting up two larger pieces of wood with the hatchet to make kindling when Jeff pulled up in her parking area.

"Good morning!" he said, jumping down from the high cab of the old pickup truck. "Looks like you're getting ready to build a fire. Need any help?"

"Not really; I've started many stoves up in Michigan. I could use more wood though," she answered. Jeff pulled out his walkie and called down to the office.

"As soon as Aaron can get the truck filled, he'll bring you a load," he said after a short conversation. "Any plans on using this side of the port?" Jeff asked.

"None whatsoever. Since no one knows I'm here, I'm not expecting any company," she replied.

"Okay, then I'll have him bring two loads. I don't want you running out." He grinned. "I'm going to be plowing much of the day. Would tonight be all right to come back and look at your new painting?" He didn't want her to forget her offer, and he certainly didn't want her to think he wasn't interested.

"That would be fine." Adele tried to keep the enthusiasm out of her voice. She was looking forward to the visit, but didn't want to seem desperate. The long talk they had over dinner had lifted her spirits. Jeff was an educated and intelligent man and she craved more of his company.

She gathered up the new kindling and set it in the sling. With additional wood coming, she decided to split up more. The activity felt good and it reminded her of her sixty-year-old mother and all the physical work she did on a daily basis.

The fire in the woodstove was blazing brightly when Adele heard someone pull into her short driveway.

"Good morning, Ma'am. You ordered some wood?"

"You must be Aaron," Adele said to the pleasant and handsome young black man.

"Yes, Ma'am. Mr. Atkins said to bring you two loads. I might not get the second load until tomorrow, though. It takes a bit of time to stack all this," Aaron replied.

"If you get it unloaded, I'll start stacking. I could use the exercise anyway," she said.

"Oh, I don't think Mr. Atkins would like that."

"Oh, I don't think Mr. Atkins has any say in what I do," she said, mimicking his words. She grinned and went back into the condo to find some gloves.

An hour and a half later, Aaron returned with the second load of wood, only to find Adele close to being done stacking what he'd already brought.

"Those are some mighty fine looking ricks, Ma'am. I can tell you've done this a time or two before."

"Yes, once or twice," she laughed. "My mom has wood heat back in Michigan and I spent many summers helping her put up her winter supply. My ricks have never fallen down," she boasted, referring to the neat, freestanding rows of cut wood. She stood and stretched. "If you unload in the same place, I will finish stacking tomorrow."

"If you don't mind, Miss Michaels, I'll finish. The boss-man pays me to do this, and you don't want me to get into trouble, do you?" Aaron said with a chuckle. "And here is a pile of newspapers and a bag of fat-wood. I'll leave them in the back here, out of your way." He slid a large covered plastic tub out of the back of the late model truck and set it against the back of the domed carport, and started unloading the rest of the split wood.

"No, I certainly don't want Mr. Atkins upset with you. And I appreciate you bringing the wood on such short notice, thank you."

Adele went back into the condo, silently thankful she didn't have to stack any more wood.

At six o'clock, Adele was beginning to wonder if Jeff forgot about stopping by. She felt an odd twinge of disappointment until she heard a knock on the door.

"I thought you might have forgotten," she said when she saw Jeff standing there.

"Forget a date with you? Never," he said softly.

A date? She felt another twinge; alarm and excitement flooded her chest. She opened the door wider to let him in and saw his plow truck.

"Isn't that truck a bit old to be plowing the roads?" she asked.

"That's a 1963 Chevy Fleet side ¾ ton 4x4, I'll have you know. It's been completely restored and runs better than the new trucks.

I love classic cars. I also have a '57 Chevy and a 1942 Willis-Jeep, both need more work though." Jeff held up two bottles of wine. "I brought a bottle of red and one of white, not sure which you prefer," he said.

"I prefer red blends, unless there is a food that needs something milder," Adele replied. "And I have only a few rules about wine: red is cool not cold, white is chilled, and a wine glass, or anything that can spill, is never set down on my art table."

"Simple rules and easy to abide by," Jeff agreed. He deftly opened the red wine and poured them each a glass. "Now, where is this new painting?"

Adele led him over to the table where it lay. Jeff walked around the table, scrutinizing the heavy paper.

"That is absolutely stunning. I get different impressions from the different angles. Which one are you going to use?"

She was impressed that he could see that. "I don't know yet. Tell me, what do you see?"

"From here the pine needles are falling, drifting downward. Yet from here…" he moved to the other side, "…I see the needles in flight, like they are on a gust of wind being carried away." He looked at her. "What do *you* see?"

She smiled broadly and turned the paper over, revealing the title, *Wind Swept*. "Are you sure you didn't sneak in here and peek?"

Jeff smiled. "Your work really is amazing, Adele. It evokes emotions."

They sat at the snack bar to drink their wine. Jeff got up once to put another log on the fire.

"Tell me more about the resort," Adele prompted. "How long have you worked here?"

He looked down into his empty glass. Before answering, he reached for the bottle of wine and refilled their glasses.

"I've been here from the start, Adele. This is *my* resort. I'm the owner. I have a degree in architecture and designed the entire compound. What you see has been a long time dream of mine."

"No wonder Aaron called you boss-man." She smiled. "Why domes? They must have been more costly to construct." She rested her chin on her palm, watching him.

"Yes and no. Since I was my own designer and builder I saved a bundle. As for why domes, they're safer for this area. I designed them for tolerating a tremendous amount of snow-load, and they've held up beyond my expectations. Nothing would ruin a vacation quicker than having the roof cave in," Jeff laughed.

"Okay, I'm taking your word on that. The power plant my mother is so afraid of: where is it and does it have any vulnerabilities?"

"Your mother?"

"My mother is a prepper and lives in the woods in the Upper Peninsula of Michigan. When she found out where I was hiding out, she was all paranoid about you losing power during the winter."

"A prepper? I've heard the term before. What did she suggest?"

"Well, when she found out this condo is all electric, she made me promise to get a camp stove to cook on, oil lamps for lighting, and lots of food. The food I had already taken care of, since I planned on not leaving here again for a minimum of six months. My last run into town was to Walstroms for the camping equipment," Adele explained.

"She sounds like a smart woman. Do you always do what she says?" Jeff asked, the corners of his mouth twitching into a smile.

38

"I have to. She knows when I'm lying to her. Besides, too many times she's been right and I should have listened. Had I listened I would have saved myself from the worst mistake of my life."

"That sounds like a story in itself," he replied. "Why don't we continue this over dinner? I think the special tonight is salmon."

"I have a better idea." Adele stood and pulled the two steaks out of the refrigerator she had thawing. "While I cook, tell me about the generator so I can quell my mother's worries."

"Well, it *is* a power plant, about the size of your bedroom. Although it's run primarily on wind power, it does have a backup propane fuel input. I try not to use the propane, partly because of cost, though mostly the unreliability of winter refills. It's located on the other side of the complex, along with the five hundred gallon gas tank for the vehicles, out of the way, and housed in their own domes for protection and for fitting in. Some consider the generators and three windmills unsightly, so they're out of the way too. All the power lines are underground so nothing can be damaged from bad weather. Both the propane and the gas tank were refilled a week ago. You can tell your mother not to worry."

"Impressive. How many times has it gone down?" she asked.

"Never."

"That was wonderful, thank you. I didn't expect to be fed," Jeff commented, rinsing their plates and setting them in the dishwasher. "So tell me about the worst mistake of your life."

"I got married."

Jeff waited for the chuckle that usually went with a statement like that. It didn't come.

"I've been divorced for almost ten months now. My mom knew Kyle was bad news right from the start. How, I don't know, because he sure had *me* fooled, until after we were married. Then he showed his violent side." Adele saw the startled and concerned look on Jeff's face. "Don't worry, not only is he locked away in a mental hospital, but no one knows exactly where I am, not my mother, not my attorney, *no* one."

"So is he why you're hiding?" Jeff asked softly, knowing he was treading into a delicate issue.

"Yes. I'm hoping that six months of intense therapy will help him, and he'll lose his obsession with me. Restraining orders haven't worked." She set her glass down. "That was probably too much information, right? Sorry, must be the wine," she paused briefly, "and the comfortable company."

Adele walked over to the woodstove and added another log. "And now that I've effectively scared you off …" She shrugged.

"Hey, Adele, I don't scare off that easily." He brushed a stray lock of hair from her face and the desire to kiss her was almost overwhelming. Almost. "On that note, I do have to get back to plowing. Thank you again for dinner. Please let me know when you've completed another painting. I've thoroughly enjoyed this private viewing."

What am I getting myself into? Jeff thought pulling away from her unit. If I weren't the boss I'd fire me.

CHAPTER EIGHT

"Ever notice how winter storms sound louder than summer storms? They're not really though. A summer storm has wind and rain, thunder and lightning, all competing for your ears. A winter storm has wind and snow, no thunder, no lightning, no pounding rain, and the snow is silent. So all you hear is the wind howling and it sounds louder because it's the only thing you *can* hear." Adele stood at the picture window staring at the swirling snow, talking to Jeff as he circled the table with three new paintings spread out.

He walked over to her desk, set his wine glass down, and went back to pick up one of the paintings. "I can't figure this one out, Adele. What is it?"

She went back to see which one had him perplexed. Ah, this was a difficult one, she thought. She took it from him and turned it once, so it was on end, and handed it back. "What do you see now?"

"This is going on a Christmas card?"

She laughed hard. "No, it's going on my wall."

"It's a... fire breathing dragon, stomping the shit out of something!"

She laughed again. "Sometimes the paintings tell *me* what they are, not the other way around." She turned it again. "I wanted it to be a log cabin in the woods at sunrise, but it had other ideas." Adele flipped it over to reveal the title: *Dragon's Breath*. "It took me ten days because I was fighting it. Those two were done in two days, while I put this one aside."

"No wonder I haven't seen much of you lately," he said, setting the painting down and retrieving his glass. "This deserves a night out!"

"In this storm?"

"It's only a little snow. You told me you don't melt, remember? Besides, the chef has something special planned for tonight."

Adele had changed into a pair of her new flannel lined pants, a turtleneck sweater, coat, hat, fur lined gloves, and tall boots for the walk down to the restaurant. While Jeff had called it only a 'little snow,' she thought of it as a light *blizzard*. He appeared unaffected by the chilling winds.

"What is the special tonight?" she asked the waiter.

"Before you answer that, Matt, check with Chet. I think he was doing something different for us tonight," Jeff interrupted.

"Yes, sir. What about a wine, Miss Michaels?" Matt asked. The staff was getting used to having her around. He had heard through the staff gossip vine that she was staying all winter, perhaps longer.

"I think we would be safe with a white, Matt." She smiled at him, thinking of how pleasant all of the personnel was toward her.

"Very good. I'll double check with Chef Chet to make sure it won't clash with whatever he's planning," he said to Jeff and departed.

"Stuffed rainbow trout? Wow, I'm impressed," Adele gushed.

"And a Caesar salad," Jeff said.

"Yes, and the Caesar salad. I love Caesar salad. You're spoiling me," she said, taking a forkful of the crabmeat-stuffed trout.

"There are advantages to being the working general manager and decision-maker. When Chet needs to try out something, I get to be the guinea pig, and that's not a complaint," he replied. "I'm going to guess too that the recent shipment of food included the fresh fish, and likely Chet froze the rest."

"I didn't notice any food trucks recently," Adele commented.

"We try to be discreet. There's a separate entrance for supply trucks. We have a walk-in freezer, walk-in cooler, and an extensive pantry. Chet likes to maintain a well-stocked pantry and freezer, and from the looks of the bills, he's about done, with the exception of fresh vegetables once a week. In December when we get busy I'll hire a baker, too. I'm pleased to say the restaurant portion of the resort has developed an excellent reputation among the locals."

"It would appear that I definitely picked the right place to come," she said.

"Considering the quality of work you've created already, I would have to agree."

"I don't see many people about, Jeff. Who is here?" Adele asked curiously.

Jeff leaned back in his chair. "You've met Aaron. He's my right arm here; an all-around handyman and excellent mechanic. Then there is Beth, and before you say anything, please accept my apology for not reminding you that housekeeping is part of what you pay for. She came to me right after that incident and told me everything. She was upset until I explained to her your desire for privacy."

"Thank you. I think we'll be okay now. Who else is here?"

"It's a skeleton staff right now, so other than Aaron and Beth, who are married, by the way, there is Matt, Chet, and myself. The first of December, the number will triple. We also have three condos still occupied, other than yours. The total people, guests and staff, are twelve. One of the couples will be leaving tomorrow."

"Is it worth staying open for so few?" Adele questioned.

"Absolutely," he replied. "Oh, and Chet insists on doing Thanksgiving dinner. It will be a private party for all the guests and staff. I know it's still a week away, but may I ask you to attend with me?"

"Like a *date*?"

"Like a date."

"I'd like that, Jeff." Adele took a sip of the buttery chardonnay to hide her grin.

After letting herself into the condo, Adele kicked off her boots, added another log to the fire, and sat down to sketch. Leaving the restaurant in the snow, Adele was mesmerized by the view of her condo up the hill.

CHAPTER NINE

Adele pushed away from the art table and stood. She circled the table once, noting the changes in the latest painting. After wetting the paper with a watered down blue, the only colors she had used after that were gray and white. The effect was nothing short of stunning. It took her five days but she decided this might be her best piece yet.

She dialed the front desk from her cellphone.

"What can I do for my lovely lady?" Jeff answered, recognizing the number.

"You can join me for dinner tonight. I have something to show you," she replied, inwardly grinning like the proverbial Cheshire cat.

"You've finished another piece? I'll be there at six!"

Jeff sighed after hanging up the phone. He was becoming very attached to his favorite resident, and wondered if that was good or bad.

Adele started a batch of spaghetti sauce from a recipe in her head that was her mother's. Simmering the rest of the day would be required to bring out all the different flavors. With the pot on the back burner of the stove, she cleaned up her art table, washing the brushes carefully and putting all but the one finished piece away in her portfolio bag. This one piece had center stage tonight.

Jeff arrived promptly at six o'clock, carrying a bottle of chilled champagne.

"It smells heavenly in here!" He breathed in the aromas. "Talented, beautiful, *and* she can cook." He handed Adele the bottle. "I'm not sure if this will go with the spaghetti I smell, but I got the impression this was a special viewing."

He kissed her chastely on the cheek.

"It is." Adele grinned. She handed the bottle of Dom Pérignon back to him to open while she removed two flutes from the overhead rack. After he poured the bubbling wine, he stepped back. She hooked her arm into his and led him to the near empty art table. Earlier she had placed a single sheet of blank paper over the finished piece. Now she removed it.

Jeff looked at the artwork, then at her, then back at the table.

"Adele..." He walked around the table, pausing on each side for a good look. He walked around a second time. "Adele. I'm speechless. Which view is the real one?"

"They all are."

They stood there looking at an almost three-dimensional rendition of the condos, as viewed from Jeff's perspective while he was at the front desk.

He walked around the table yet again, admiring the gray and white snowy picture. "Will you never cease to amaze me? This is beyond beautiful, it's... *alive*."

"And it's yours," she said quietly.

He took her wine glass from her and set it on the island next to his. Turning back to her, he pulled her into his arms and kissed her gently, then deeply.

"I can't accept the painting."

"You'd better. I made it for you."

"But—"

Adele looked hurt. "Would you really reject something I'm freely offering to you that came from my heart?"

"No, not when you put it that way."

She ran her fingers through his hair and pulled him closer. Their eyes locked and their lips met again.

CHAPTER TEN

Jeff called Adele from the front desk where he was busy doing paperwork and paying bills on the computer. He called rather than stop in to see her. After the other night, he couldn't get her off his mind and he was afraid he wouldn't be able to keep his hands off her if they were alone. Their evening had been erotic, made more so by remaining chaste.

"You do know what today is, don't you?"

"Well now, let's see. It's Thursday, right?" she replied with a chuckle.

"Yes, it is."

"Oh, I know! It's a Thursday so I don't have to cook!"

"You are being cruel to me," Jeff said, feigning being crushed by her words.

Adele laughed. "What time is dinner?"

"How about I pick you up at four o'clock?"

"I can walk down. Considering that chef of yours, I might need to walk several miles to wear off the feast I hear he's creating."

"Okay, but I insist on escorting you home."

"Deal."

CHAPTER ELEVEN

"I'm only being honest with you, Kyle, and as your attorney, I'm suggesting you listen to me and listen closely," Colin Jones stated. He sat in the same chair across from Kyle Polez as Adele had. While he didn't particularly like his client, he paid well and always on time.

"I'm listening, but you better be working on a way to get me out of here or you're fired," Kyle sulked.

"I am, but you have to help," Colin leaned forward on his elbows. "Adele won't budge on dropping the charges. You were supposed to leave her alone. Instead you tried to abduct her and you broke her arm in the process. The judge is not looking at that as you being rehabilitated."

"She's my wife!" Kyle slapped the table hard, and the guard at the door went on alert. Taking note, Kyle dropped his voice to a whisper. "I was only trying to get her to come home where she belongs."

"By the ruling of a judge in the state of Texas, Adele is no longer your wife. She divorced you legally over ten months ago. The only way you have of ever making up with her, and getting out of here, is to be a model patient. Go to therapy, take your meds, and show the good state of Texas you are no longer an anger risk." Colin eyed his client. He could see the anger and violence hovering just below the surface. "Can you do that, Kyle? Can you pretend long enough to get out of here?" Colin had set the hook.

"Yeah, I can do that," Kyle replied. And when I get out of here I'm going to find that bitch and kill her for putting me through this.

Six weeks later, millionaire Kyle Polez stepped past the keyless gates and slid into the backseat of his limo.

"Take me to my office," he demanded of his driver. "Please."

Kyle ran his hands over the soft leather of his chair. From behind his desk he could see the entire office, but because of the one-way tint, his staff couldn't see him watching them. He pushed a button and closed the drapery, and then buzzed his secretary.

"Marjory, would you please ask Seth Miller to come in here? Thank you." It was hard to be so nice to the people he detested. They served a function for him and he would tolerate his new image, at least until the ankle monitor came off.

"Welcome back, Mr. Polez," Seth said, holding a file in his hands. He waited with a smile until his boss invited him to sit.

"Thank you, Seth. Have a seat. What can you tell me about Adele's activities over the last two months?" Kyle said, getting right to the point.

Seth opened the file and handed Kyle the first sheet of paper. "I've kept a close eye on the tracking device in her Lexus. When it didn't move for a week I followed the beacon to a dealership. She left it there on consignment. I haven't found any vehicle registered to her since."

Kyle stared at the information. "She sold my gift to her? How unkind of her. What else?" It was getting harder to maintain control on his temper, now that he was off those stupid drugs the hospital forced on him.

"Her cellphone hasn't been used, and neither has her computer," Seth continued. Kyle scowled. His company was founded on computer hacking. He was hired to hack a system, find all the flaws, and fix them, for a healthy fee. He fixed them, and he always left a backdoor so *he* could get back in. What good was it if he couldn't use that backdoor to help him find *one* person?

"However," Seth continued, "I put a trace on her bank accounts, and while we can't manipulate them, we can monitor the activity." Kyle looked up. "She's in Montana, sir. I can't pinpoint exactly where, because she hasn't used her cards wherever she is staying, but she's been to Butte to shop, then to the small town of Avon, then a week later back to Butte, and again to Avon. She hasn't used any credit cards, only the debit, which most don't realize can be traced just like credit cards. By the types of purchases to her debit card, she's somewhere in Avon, Montana."

Kyle smiled.

CHAPTER TWELVE

Adele put two more logs on the fire, hoping to keep the coals going while she was at the Thanksgiving dinner. She dressed in a long blue and green plaid skirt with deep green silk long-johns underneath and a dark green turtleneck sweater. She decided on the low heeled boots that would give her more stability in her walk to the restaurant. It was snowing again, and she should have let Jeff pick her up.

The long scarf wrapped around her head and neck kept the wind out, and the knee length down coat kept her warm enough, but she still felt a chill. Winter had arrived in Montana.

Adele closed her door and set off on her trek down to the gathering. Five steps outside, her cellphone rang quietly and she missed the call from her attorney.

"Adele, it's Anthony Evers. I just got word that Kyle was let out of the hospital last week, and three days ago he slipped his electronic tether. So much for the courts giving us advanced warning! Please be extra careful!" was the message left on her voice mail.

Jeff met Adele at the front door of the restaurant. Although he had been spending extra time with her and he was sure the staff had noticed, he still didn't want to make it obvious their relationship was evolving and growing more intimate. They hadn't stepped over that line, though it was getting close. The restraint was intoxicating to him.

"Let me take your coat," he said, hanging it by the door on the clothes racks. In another couple of weeks, it would be filled with ski jackets and heavy boots. "You look lovely tonight." He kissed her cheek and led her over to the tables they would share with the other dozen people in attendance.

"How festive it all looks, Jeff!" Adele took in the green and white candles that were placed by every person. The long table linens were deep beige, and the cranberry, green, and matching beige napkins were a perfect accent. The crystal sparkled in the soft light emitted by the fireplace behind them.

Matt came by and poured everyone a glass a champagne, a signal to Jeff that everyone who was invited had arrived and was seated.

"I'll be right back," Jeff whispered to Adele. The tables had been arranged in a tight U-shape, to allow easy access by the working staff, yet close enough that conversation with anyone was possible. Jeff made his way to the center and picked up his glass.

"Good evening everyone, and Happy Thanksgiving! I'm delighted you could join me in this festive meal. The Geo Dome Resort opens again in one week, on December 1st, and there won't be many more occasions for this kind of cozy dinner, so enjoy yourself." He raised his glass to them and took a sip. "And now I would like to introduce everyone, since some of our guests haven't met yet." Jeff started at the furthest end of the table and gave everyone's first name only. This was the solution he had pondered when it came to Adele. Someone might recognize her full name. He had promised to keep her secret and he fully intended to do that.

Course after course was served on alternating buffet tables. The working staff, Beth and Matt, were being paid triple time, and were there to keep dishes cleared away and to keep wine bottles replaced as they were emptied. When not busy, they each sat and enjoyed the meal.

The atmosphere was jovial and festive. Adele was relaxed and enjoying herself, until she heard someone calling her name.

"Adele, I understand you're going to be here all winter," Gwen Swanson said, "what do you do that you can take that much time off?" The question was innocent, yet it sent a wave of panic coursing through Adele.

She smiled to stall for time. "Oh, I don't do anything, Gwen. I'm a TFB." The lie was met with silence at first.

"What is that?"

"A Trust Fund Baby. Daddy was a rich man," Adele answered.

"What did *he* do?" Gwen pushed.

"I'm not at liberty to discuss that," Adele retorted. "Family secrets, you know?" She added a laugh. The conversation drifted away from her.

Jeff leaned closer. "That was a good dodge." He could smell her hair and it smelled of sunshine, which they hadn't seen for days.

The dessert table had just been set with an array of sweets when the lights went out, leaving everyone basking in candlelight.

There were a few gasps around the room at the suddenness of the dark. With candles glowing around the room, shadows danced and flickered, creating movement that wasn't there.

"I'm on it," Aaron said to Jeff, pushing his chair back. He pulled a flashlight from his pocket and switched it on. "Hmm, new LED flashlight, fresh batteries, and the darn thing won't work."

"There's another one on the front desk," Jeff said. "I'll get it." He grabbed a candle and made his way down the dark hall with Aaron following him. The flashlight was right where it was supposed to be; however, it didn't work either. "This is confusing, Aaron. I know this was good this morning, I used it to look for something under the desk."

Aaron had a worried look on his face, and pulled out his cell phone. "Cellphone isn't working either. I think we have a really big problem on our hands, boss-man." They both noticed a light coming down the dark hallway.

"Is everything alright?" Adele asked.

"How come your flashlight works and ours don't?" Jeff queried.

"May I see your light, ma'am?" Aaron asked politely. When Adele handed it to him, she moved closer to Jeff and waited. "This isn't an LED, it's an older style. Battery engages bulb when the button is pushed, a simple design." He handed it back. "Can I talk to you privately, Jeff?"

"Jeff, I'll wait for you back at the table," Adele said.

When they were alone, Jeff faced his trusted friend and employee. "What's on your mind, Aaron? What do you think is going on?"

"I don't know, Jeff, and I don't want to speculate without knowing more. If we don't have any working lights, I can't check out the power plant until the morning, and maybe not even then... unless your girlfriend will loan me her light," Aaron said.

"My girlfriend?"

"Come on, Jeff, I'm not blind. The whole staff knows you've been spending a lot of time with Adele. Don't worry, we also think it's great, and she seems like a really nice person, so we're happy for you," Aaron reassured him.

Jeff blew out a breath through his pursed lips. "Okay, let's not make a big deal out of it. Back to the problem at hand, I'll ask her about the flashlight. Still, why does her light work and ours don't?"

"Hers is an older one. LEDs have a substrate composed of gallium arsenide, a semi-conductor, but it's enough to make them vulnerable to certain problems." Aaron paced a bit, and then came back into the candlelight. "What time is it?"

Jeff looked at his watch and frowned. "My watch stopped."

"Mine too. I'm betting all the computers don't work either, even the laptops with a fully charged battery."

Jeff waited while Aaron paced again.

"Shit." He looked toward his boss. "I think we've been hit with some kind an EMP, maybe a massive solar flare. If that's happened and *we're* out, then maybe *everyone* is out."

"An electromagnetic pulse? How would we know for sure?" Jeff asked.

"We try turning on anything that should run without being plugged in," Aaron suggested.

"If that's what has really happened, we're in a world of hurt, aren't we?" Jeff looked off toward the restaurant. "Let's not alarm everyone yet until we know for sure, okay? What else can we test?"

"A car!" Aaron snapped his fingers. "There are so many electronics and computers in a car now, it wouldn't stand a chance."

"The truck is right outside; let's try it." Jeff headed to the door.

"Wait, Jeff. That's a 1963, made before all the electronic parts went into a vehicle. It might be the only thing running here, or anywhere else in the state."

"It might take a while to get the generator working again," Jeff announced. "But we've got plenty of candles and dessert to eat!"

He sat back down next to Adele and leaned toward her. "What kind of batteries does your flashlight take?" he asked quietly.

"AA, why?"

"I may have to borrow it later."

Adele looked at him askance.

"We'll talk more when I take you home."

"I think everyone walked down. If any of you want a ride back to your dome, I'll be happy to do that," Jeff offered. It was a beautiful moonlit night and most decided to walk. Jeff opened the plow truck door for Adele to climb in.

"I'll take you home first, Adele. If it's okay, after I take Lane and Gwen home I'll stop back. It will give me a chance to talk to you about what may be going on."

Jeff returned to Adele's unit ten minutes later and was surprised to see a light in the window. He knocked on her door. When she opened it, he saw what was creating the light.

"Are you always this prepared?" he asked, admiring the oil lamps on the counter.

"No, but my mother-the-prepper insists on me having certain things with me *all* the time, and as I said before I swear she would know if I didn't!" Adele laughed. "While you were taking Lane and Gwen home, I checked my voicemail."

"And?" Jeff asked hopefully.

"My phone doesn't work. I know it had a full charge, too. And the TV doesn't work, but that needs power."

"Have you tried booting up your laptop?" he asked cautiously.

Adele took one of the oil lamps over to the desk where her computer was and turned it on. "Nothing." She scowled. "Jeff, what is going on?"

He took her by the shoulders and looked into her eyes. "Aaron thinks it might have been a solar flare, and it's taken out the grid."

"A solar flare big enough to take out the grid, would take out all electronics, yes," Adele thought out loud. "We also should have been given some notice. Those X-Class flares take a couple of days to reach the Earth. They don't sneak up on us anymore." She noticed Jeff giving her a strange look. "I read a lot."

Kyle stopped at a diner in the small town of Avon for dinner. The special was turkey, and the waitress cheerfully wished him a Happy

Thanksgiving. Kyle hated turkey and ordered a burger. He didn't want to leave her a tip for being so chipper, but no tip or even a big tip would be remembered, and he didn't want to be remembered. He left an adequate amount of cash and left to find a gas station and a motel. He had been driving all day and was exhausted. Tomorrow he would find that place Adele bought all the clothes and get some answers.

CHAPTER THIRTEEN

Jeff and Aaron stepped out of the old pickup truck and knocked on Adele's door. Looking a little confused, she opened the door to the two of them.

"Care for some coffee?" she offered.

"What? How did you make coffee?" Aaron asked.

"I heated water on the woodstove and used my French press. There are lots of ways of doing simple things, with or without power." They sat sipping coffee and discussing events.

"Okay, if not a solar flare, then what? And have you tried starting your car yet, Miss Michaels? It's new, and probably has a few circuit boards," Aaron said.

"A few circuit boards?" She laughed. "That car is loaded. Let's go try it." Adele grabbed her keys and led them to the carport.

"Nada, not even a blinking light," Adele got out of the dead car, and they went back inside to the warmth of the woodstove.

"Would a solar flare really cause that much damage to the grid?" Jeff asked.

"I really don't know," she confessed. "What if it wasn't a solar flare? What if it was something intentional... like a high-yield nuke?"

Aaron started. "You think someone *nuked* us?"

"I don't think anything yet. Isn't it a possibility, though?" Adele thought back to the newscast she heard. "It wasn't that long ago there was a news report about North Korea arming a missile with a nuclear warhead, followed by the bobble-heads suggesting sanctions against them."

"They wouldn't care two wits about sanctions. They hate us, plain and simple, and if our grid went down, our government wouldn't be able to enforce sanctions anyway," Aaron replied.

Jeff looked back and forth between the two. "I think I'm really glad to have two really smart people on my side. What do we do now?"

"It might be a good idea for one of you to go into Avon and see if anyone else is affected," Adele suggested. "If it's only the resort, then it's something else."

With sun streaming through the massive glass windows, Adele pushed her art table closer for more of the natural light. She took all of the finished paintings except for *Dragon's Breath* and the untitled dome one, and put them in one of the canvas portfolio bags she carried with her at all times. She put the bag in her closet out of the way.

Now she didn't feel so cluttered. Adele took a new sheet and created a washed background, then another, and another. Six sheets later she went back to the first one and spread fern leaves in a random pattern, moving them around until she was satisfied. She worked for hours, forgetting lunch and occasionally wondering what Jeff may have found out by going into town.

"I'm telling ya, Jeff, if Avon is down too, people are going to get real twitchy when they see you've got a working car," Aaron pointed out.

"Are you saying we shouldn't go?"

"Not at all, though I think we should be taking one of those shotguns I know you have. Just in case."

The ride into town was slow and uneventful. There were no tire tracks in the snow from the previous night; no plows had been by; no mail delivery. The few houses along the ten mile route were silent and dark.

Approaching the edge of Avon, Jeff stopped the truck to observe. "I don't like the looks of this," he said. "There is nothing moving, and it's so quiet."

"May I make a suggestion, boss-man?" Aaron asked. "Park the truck over there and let's walk. Being on foot will be a lot less conspicuous than driving around." Aaron pointed to a parking lot in front of the Mountain View Motel where there were a few other cars. They slid the shotgun and a rifle under the wide front seat, and Jeff locked the truck, pocketing the keys.

"The township's and sheriff's office are two blocks down. I say we start with those," Jeff suggested. They passed the dark and silent traffic light. Three cars had been in an accident and still sat in the middle of the road. The café was dark, although they could see a few people sitting at the counter. Everything else was closed.

The front door to the township government building opened easily and they stepped into the dim and cold room. The sheriff, still wearing his heavy dark gray wool jacket and insulated leather gloves, stepped out to see who had come in.

"Jeff, Aaron, good to see you," Sheriff Claude Burns said when he recognized his visitors. He was a tall man, six foot three, and not as lean as he used to be. At fifty years old, his short dark brown hair was starting to show some gray at the temples, and his gray eyes required readers for the fine print these days.

"Sheriff," Jeff acknowledged. "Do you have any idea what is going on? The resort lost all power last night, and by the looks of the town, so have you."

"Yeah, everything stopped around seven o'clock last night," Claude said. "Not only is the power out, cars won't run, phones don't work, nothing. Most people are staying inside trying to keep warm. A few are lucky enough to have wood heat, though not many."

"This morning I tracked down that retired professor that moved here a few years back to see if he could shed any light on this. Forgive the pun," he chuckled. "He thinks we're experiencing the effects of an EMP, but with everything down, there's no way to find out. It's a conundrum."

"You know we're not on grid power up at the resort, but even our generator won't work," Aaron said.

"Same here," Claude remarked. "I just got back from checking with Nathan, the guy with the ham radio."

"I remember when there was a big ruckus over his huge tower."

"Yep, that's the guy. His setup is new and fancy, and is totally fried. Even his back up gennie is toast. Although, he said he was talking with someone on the West Coast right before this happened," Claude continued, "and the TV had a breaking news flash that said three missiles were launched at us from the Pacific somewhere and then everything went down."

Jeff and Aaron looked at each other.

"What are you going to do, Claude? What will happen to everyone here?" Jeff asked.

"These are good people. We'll all pull together and ride this out. If I can make a suggestion though, I'd get back to the resort and stay put if you can," the sheriff said.

"That's good advice, Claude. You take care now."

Jeff and Aaron shook hands with the sheriff and left.

Kyle woke early, as he always did, noticing his clock was out. Even in the hospital he woke early although they wouldn't let him have internet access, his computer, or anything else. He turned on his state of the art laptop that he built and programmed himself and dressed while it was booting up, only it didn't. With his anger issues resurfacing, he almost threw it against the wall before thinking that this backwoods town likely didn't have a computer store for him to replace it, and he tossed it on the bed instead.

Kyle sat in his new Explorer, trying to start it. "Damn piece of junk!" he said, slapping the steering wheel. Movement caught his attention and he watched two men, one white, and one black, get into an old truck and drive away.

He walked down to the café where he had dinner the night before for some breakfast, only to find it dark and cold inside.

"Is the power out everywhere in this damn town?" Kyle said to the first person he saw. "And is there a halfway decent mechanic here? My car won't start!" he grumbled.

The guy looked at Kyle in distain for his rudeness and said, "Yes, yes, and no one's will." He went back to his cooling coffee.

"What is that supposed to mean?" Kyle snarled.

"It means, yes, the power is out everywhere in town; yes, we have a good mechanic; and it won't do you any good because *no one's* car will start," the waitress replied. "We do have a single gas burner that works and I can give you some hot coffee."

Kyle was stunned. Something was very wrong. As a computer expert he knew all the things computers were vulnerable to, and this one made him nervous. He took a steadying breath to check his mounting anger and sat at the counter. "Thank you, coffee would be good."

Mae, the waitress, picked up his empty cup after he left, along with a reasonable tip and a Juicy Fruit gum wrapper.

CHAPTER FOURTEEN

Jeff tapped on Adele's door.

"Well, that's a glum look if I've ever seen one," she said when she opened it to see him standing there. "What's wrong, Jeff?"

"You were right."

"About what?"

"There were three missiles launched at the U.S. last night, right before everything shut down," Jeff explained. "We got nuked."

"Three?" Adele gasped. "North Korea?"

"I don't know. There apparently was a brief ham radio message sent, and then it was gone. You said you read a lot. What do you know about nukes and EMPs?"

"Only that if a nuclear bomb is set off at a high altitude, which technically makes it an NEMP, a Nuclear Electromagnetic Pulse, the wavelength it puts out covers a great deal of area and instantly destroys electronic circuitry. Maybe then it's a HEMP, a High-altitude EMP, I'm not sure. One bomb would cover a lot of area, but three… three would knock us back a hundred and fifty years. It was one of those near-impossible events that my mother always talked about, and why she had manual backups for nearly everything: oil lamps for lighting, a wood cookstove for heat and cooking, a hand pump on her well, things like that. She believes an EMP would affect everyone."

"You think the whole country could be out?" Jeff asked, astonished.

"I don't know, Jeff, I really don't. It was an interesting article, that's all, and I only half listened to what my mother said. I didn't do any research on it, if that's what you're thinking." Adele walked over to the woodstove and put another log on the fire, bringing the coffeepot back and poured Jeff a cup of the black brew. "Oh, I found something you might be able to use."

From her bedroom closet, Adele brought out a battery operated lantern and handed it to Jeff. "Aaron might find it better to use than my little flashlight."

He smiled at her. "Have I told you yet today how amazing you are?" He switched the lamp on and grinned at how bright the light was. "I'm going to get this to Aaron, and then I'm going to visit each condo and organize a meeting for later."

"What time?" Adele asked.

"About an hour, but watches have stopped working too."

Adele looked at her wrist. "It's three o'clock."

"Your watch works?" Jeff said surprised.

"My mom gave me this years ago. It was hers as a girl." She held out her arm and showed him her Cinderella watch. "I have to remember to wind it every morning." Jeff laughed, delighted. "I'll see you at the restaurant in one hour," he said, still smiling.

The twelve people sat around two tables that had been pushed together in front of the windows for the fading light. Chef Chet had made sandwiches and set them in the center, while Matt passed out bottles of water. They may have had a feast the night before, but everyone was naturally hungry again.

Jeff explained what they had found out in Avon.

"So what does that mean to us? When is the power coming back on?" Nancy Bjork asked, clutching her husband Bill's hand.

"I have no idea when the power is coming back, Nancy," Jeff said. "Our electricity here is from the resort power plant. Aaron is doing what he can to see if he can repair it, but it's not looking good. He said the circuits are fused in the inverter." He looked around the table. "As for what it means to us, I don't know that either. We have limited resources. What I *can* do is offer anyone who wants to go to Avon a ride into town. Maybe they can do better for you."

"How is it that your car works when ours don't?" demanded Marvin Jenkins.

"It's a really old truck that doesn't have any electronics built into it. Like I said, I can get you into Avon and after that, they can help you. I think that might be a good option for most of you," Jeff answered.

Kyle walked back to the motel as it started snowing again. He'd gleaned some information from the locals, and had a better grasp of what was going on, but it didn't help. He kicked the snow off his loafers and opened his motel room door. Housekeeping had been by, made the bed, and left two extra blankets.

He stood looking out the single window and remembered the old truck, wondering where they had gone. It was too late in the day, but maybe tomorrow he could follow the tracks and talk those guys into selling him that old rattletrap.

"Are you going or staying, Adele?" Jeff asked tentatively.

"I have no place to go, Jeff, and couldn't get there if I did. I think I'll stay here. I have food, water, heat and… company. Why would I want to leave?"

He took her hands. "I'm glad. In fact, I'm delighted. What you said makes me think though. If this lasts a long time, we might run out of food."

"Didn't you tell me the kitchen had already stocked for the winter? That was for a lot of guests. If there are only a few of us, it should last a long time."

He nodded. "We need another meeting, one with only the employees… and you." He hugged her and lightly brushed his lips across hers.

"So here's the deal," Jeff said to his employees, "we might have enough food to last the six of us perhaps six months, less if any of the guests decide to stay. There is only one couple undecided about leaving, the Swansons. The other two I'm taking into town in the morning. Adele is staying."

"What do you want us to do, Jeff?" Beth asked.

"Without the central electric heating, we will have to group to conserve wood for burning," Jeff said, thinking out loud.

"The first dome up the hill is a two bedroom," Beth said. "I think the four of us can stay there, and like all the single domes, it has a woodstove like Miss Michaels' place." The insinuation that Jeff would be staying with Adele hung silently in the air.

"Without heat, I'll have to drain pipes in all units not being used," Aaron said, "or we'll have a real mess on our hands come spring. We might anyway, depending on how cold the winter gets."

"Make that your top priority," Jeff said looking at Aaron. "The next, of course, will be to keep working on the generator. How is that coming along?"

"Not good. However, I've got some ideas that may or may not work that could restore limited electricity."

"Keep me updated." Jeff faced Matt and Chet. "What's the situation with food and water?"

"It's only a guess, mind you, but I think if we ration we can get those six months out of what we have," Chet informed him. "The biggest issue will be what's in the freezers. Without power it will start to thaw."

Adele spoke up for the first time. "My mother has a saying: why try to keep something at forty degrees *inside*, when it's forty degrees *outside*? And it's getting colder every day."

"Smart mom," Chet said. "When I start to notice a thaw I can pack a lot of the freezer meats in plastic bags and bury them in the snow or in one of the unused units when it gets cold enough. That should buy us some time. Meanwhile, I suggest we eat mostly from the freezer instead of the dry pantry."

"The bottled water is a different situation," Matt added. "We've got a lot, but not enough for six months. We do have snow we can melt. We should also try to keep the water from freezing, since it would burst the bottles. I can move it to the two places if it starts to freeze in here."

"I like these ideas," Jeff said. "What else?"

"Since it's already getting cold in here, I think I should ready that unit as soon as the Jenkins are out," Beth offered. "I'll collect all the extra blankets and have them readily available."

"Thanks, Beth. I'm taking them into town tomorrow morning. In the meantime, I'll load up wood in the truck and drop some at the two places." When Aaron started to protest, Jeff said, "You have your work cut out already, Aaron: the water lines and the generator. I can do this."

Adele moved several armloads of wood into the condo near the woodstove, creating a neat pile. She was collecting another armful when Jeff backed the truck into her drive.

"Before you start unloading, how much is at the other unit? I have enough for a couple of weeks. Maybe you should fill theirs first," Adele said.

"Okay. Before I do that though, I think we should talk."

Adele set the wood she was carrying beside the fire and turned to Jeff, who had followed her inside.

"That was rather awkward, I know." He ran his hands down her arms just to touch her and laughed nervously. "I think my crew knew how I felt about you before I did."

"Stop, Jeff," she said gently. "I think it was inevitable that we would end up together, and I'm not complaining. It's sooner than I thought, though who could anticipate an EMP throwing us closer so quickly?" She stroked his cheek and kissed him lightly. "I'll meet you at the other unit and start stacking."

"You don't have to do that," he protested.

"No, I don't, but I want to and I'm good at it. We are *all* going to have to pitch in and pull our own weight now. I'm not going to sit on the sidelines and watch everyone else work when I'm perfectly capable of helping."

They finished stacking the second load of wood and walked hand in hand down to the restaurant where Chet had promised a big dinner as a final supper for the guests.

"How is Chet cooking?" Gwen asked, eying the big bowl of steaming spaghetti and meatballs. Frozen garlic bread had been thawed and a couple of bottles of red wine were placed on the tables.

"There is one gas burner that I can light with a match that is usually saved for grilling steaks. It took some rotating of the pots to cook, and the chafing pans keep everything hot with sterno," Chet informed them all. "Cooking this way is not going to be easy and the propane will definitely run out, maybe soon."

Jeff stood with his wine glass. "To our last meal together." He raised his glass toward his guests. "It's been a delight having you here. While I wish our parting was under better circumstances, I sincerely believe you will all be better off in town. Please pack tonight, as we leave at first light." He sat down next to Adele and whispered to her, "I hope I'm not sending them into a bad situation."

"Just because they booked accommodations with you doesn't mean you are responsible for them forever," she whispered back.

"For what it's worth, Jeff, I plan on using everything I have stocked before taking any of the resort's food."

"That isn't necessary."

"It is for me." She cut a tiny meatball in half, speared it, swirled it in the sauce, ate one half, and playfully fed the other half to him.

CHAPTER FIFTEEN

"Have you got everything?" Jeff asked Marvin and Mary Jenkins. They nodded. "And you two?" he asked of Bill and Nancy Bjork. The back of the truck was full of suitcases and boxes. "Unfortunately, there's only room for three of us in the cab, so the men will have to ride in the back. I promise to go easy on the potholes." He was trying to keep it light, though that's not the way he felt. Deep inside, he was afraid he was sending these nice people to their doom.

The ten mile trip took over forty minutes because of the deeper snow and fallen tree branches. When Jeff got to the edge of town, he went straight to the town hall and dropped off the four people and their luggage.

Kyle saw the old pickup truck pass the motel and stop at the government building. He set out on foot to intercept the driver.

Before he could stop the truck, the driver went right past him and disappeared up that same road. His anger surging again, he closed his eyes and took a couple of deep breaths like his therapist had taught him. When he opened them again, he spotted the Wilderness Outfitters and thought it was a serendipitous sign.

He entered the store, noting that although it was chilly, it was warmer than outside.

"Welcome, is there something I can help you with?" asked Henry, the elderly man behind the counter.

"Well, old man, I need some boots," Kyle said, even though he could see the name tag reading 'Henry'. "And maybe a warmer jacket; I wasn't prepared for being stuck here."

Henry squared his shoulders at the obvious insult, reminding himself that the customer was always right. Well, until they crossed a certain line, and then he didn't care.

"Boots are to your left, jackets are in the far right corner of the store," Henry replied with a forced smile and moved to put another log in the old woodstove that had been mostly decoration until a few days ago when the furnace quit working.

Twenty minutes later, Kyle dumped his selections on the counter and pulled out his credit card. Henry started to hand write a receipt.

"I'm sorry, sir, without power I can't take your card. Until things are restored, it's cash only, orders from the store owner," Henry said with a touch of sorrow. Even though *he* was the store owner it sounded better that way. Something about this man had him on edge and it was an instant decision to also *not* tell him what he was buying was inadequate for the weather that was coming. Hopefully this rude man would be gone by then and it wouldn't matter.

Kyle put his card away and pulled out several one hundred dollar bills to pay for his purchases. When Henry smiled, he asked, "By the way, do you happen to remember a pretty blonde woman from a couple of weeks ago? She made a rather large purchase here."

Henry disliked this man intensely and the question set off red flags. He made a show of thinking and then replied, "No, I can't say that I do. Then again, I'm only part time. Sorry." Henry made change and bagged Kyle's items.

When Kyle left the store, Henry sat heavily on the stool behind the register hoping fervently that he never found that nice Miss Michaels. Any reason that arrogant ass had to be looking for her wasn't good enough to betray her.

Back in his motel room, Kyle kicked off his wet loafers and put on his new boots over his damp socks. He carefully draped his expensive lightweight jacket over the old wooden chair and slipped on the new fiber-filled ski jacket, pulling the hood up. He looked in the mirror, thought it looked stupid, and he pushed the hood off. He headed outside toward the offices where the pickup truck driver had been and within moments of leaving his room, his short hair had a layer of snow. Kyle spotted the four people pulling their luggage along the snow rutted sidewalk coming toward him. Being the opportunist he was, he said, "That's a lot to carry, could you use some help? Where are you going?"

"That's very generous of you, young man," Marvin Jenkins said. "We're trying to find the Mountain View Motel. Do you know where that is?"

"I certainly do!" Kyle forced a smile, taking a couple of boxes. "Where did you come from?" he asked innocently.

"We were staying at the Geo Dome Resort," Nancy Bjork replied. "We were scheduled to leave in a few days anyway, but when the power went out, the manager suggested we leave today and come here. He said we would be better off, but I don't know now…"

"You walked from there?" Kyle feigned astonishment.

"Oh, no! The manager has an old truck that still runs and he drove us. He really is a nice young man," Mary Jenkins said.

"So the place is empty now?" Kyle pushed as gently as his temperament could handle. He set the boxes down carefully on the dingy tile floor of the motel office and helped set the suitcases in a neat row, trying hard not to show his intense interest in their answers.

"Well there's the staff, and the Swansons, and a nice young lady still there, though they may be coming to town too. There wasn't enough room in the truck for all of us," Nancy continued.

"I don't think Adele is in any hurry to leave," Mary said to Nancy and chuckled. They passed a knowing wink between them that Kyle missed.

ADELE!

He'd found her.

After leaving the two couples in the motel office, Kyle set out on foot following the tire tracks in the snow once he was sure of the road. Since it was the only road leading out of town that had tracks, he was sure it was the right one. About the only good that came out of his six weeks in that damn hospital was that they encouraged using the exercise equipment to work off stress. He never felt stronger or fitter. The long walk should be a piece of cake for him.

Two hours after Kyle began his trek, he began to tire. He wasn't cold—the exercise kept him warm—but he was hungry and thirsty and he brought only one bottle of water with him. He sat on a log by the side of the road to rest and downed half the bottle.

Long walk long rest; short walk short rest. The saying flitted through his mind and he couldn't remember which writer had penned that phrase in a wilderness story. He decided the walk had been short, so the rest would be short. After twenty minutes he was on his feet again, fueled by the thought of confronting Adele.

He twice slipped on the ice and fell, banging his knee on an unseen rock. He took an extra break to massage his injured knee.

Another two hours, another break. "How far is this damn place?" he said aloud. Kyle had come eight miles of the ten mile road, making two miles an hour, slow but steady progress in the deep snow. He was fatigued and dehydrated and his calves were cramping. "She will pay for putting me through this!" he yelled to the nearby pileated woodpecker, who took flight at the intrusion. He didn't know how close he was.

"I'm almost done with the cleaning of the unit, Jeff," Beth said, coming out of the recently vacated dome. "It's going slower without having a vacuum. A *lot* slower. It's a good thing most of these floors are tiled or wood and I can sweep them." She dumped the laundry bag filled with sheets and towels into the bed of the truck. "I still have to make the beds, but the rest of the place is ready. Do you think I should make a fire now?"

Jeff had finished unloading the second pile of split wood into the carport, and Adele was busy stacking. "That would be good, Beth.

I'll bring some more wood inside so you can keep the fire going and warm the place up," he answered. "Matt and Chet will be here soon to unload some of their things, and Chet has a sled filled with food supplies ready. After I load up more wood and drop it at Adele's, I'll make the truck available to them."

"Great," Beth said with a sigh.

"What's the matter, Beth?"

"I don't know. This would be an interesting adventure if there wasn't such finality to it. Know what I mean?"

"I think I do. We can only take it one day at time though," he replied. "Next week something might change, or maybe next month. Either way, we still need to get ourselves ready for the rest of the winter, unless…" he stopped and looked at her, "unless you and Aaron want to go to town?"

"Oh, no! We would never abandon you, Jeff! It's just a weird feeling, that's all." She went back into the pale gray cement dome.

"There, that's done," Adele said to Jeff, placing the last log on top of the neat piles of wood.

"I need to fill the truck one last time for today to replenish *your* supply. I'll be up in a half hour or so," Jeff answered. Adele trudged up the slight grade to her unit alone, being extra careful where she stepped. Any injury now could be disastrous.

CHAPTER SIXTEEN

Kyle approached the wooden split rail fencing and smiled at the rustic sign with modern lettering. The "Geo Dome Resort" sign was partially buried in the snow and he almost missed it. By the position of the sun it was close to five in the evening and the daylight was fading. He had been walking for nearly eight hours. He was past feeling tired.

Sticking to the shadows, Kyle inched his way up the narrow road, noting the old pickup truck backed into the drive at the dome past what he presumed to be the offices near the front. Fortunately for him there were plenty of trees and evergreen shrubs to hide behind. Once beyond the activity going on at that dome, he darted across the road to the next dome and peered at the license plate of the car still parked there. Minnesota. He made his way to the next one. The Bentley had plates from California. Frustrated, he almost stepped out of the car shelter when the pickup pulled out and headed up the hill behind him. He took a deep breath to steady his anger and dashed up to the next dome.

The dark maroon Tahoe sat silent in the carport. Kyle grinned at the Texas plates. He boldly walked up to the door of the dome and opened it, sliding silently inside.

He roamed the few rooms and was initially disappointed to find Adele was not there. He lingered in the bedroom going through her drawers and closet. When he found her 9mm pistol in the nightstand, he picked it up, checked the magazine, and, finding it full, slipped the gun into his jacket pocket.

Kyle opened the refrigerator and took out a bottle of water. He chugged it and sighed with contentment, then took another. The freezer was well stocked with all the things he knew Adele enjoyed. When he spotted the wine rack and checked the labels, he was sure this was her place. Did she really think she could hide from him that easily? He popped a stick of gum into his mouth and tossed the wrapper on the floor.

On her art table by the window he found several paintings in progress. He picked them up one at a time and tore them into pieces, taking a handful of the shreds and throwing them into the fire that was blazing in the woodstove. He heard the door open and put his back to the wall by the stove, barely out of obvious sight.

Adele tossed her leather gloves at the kitchen island and shrugged off her jacket. She had several minutes before Jeff returned with the load of wood for her. Her heart raced at the thought of what the evening might hold. One of her gloves had fallen to the floor and she stooped to pick it up. The small piece of silver paper caught her eye. When she picked it up, she got a whiff of Juicy Fruit and froze.

"Aren't you going to say hello to your husband?" Kyle asked, pushing off from the wall into full view.

Adele slowly turned toward the voice. "What are you doing here, Kyle?"

"Did you really think you could hide from me, sweetie?" he said, feeling the anger at her indifference toward him. "And didn't I tell you to *stop* painting? Why do you keep disobeying me?" he yelled, spittle flying from his mouth.

Adele's eyes darted to her art table and she saw the pile of shredded colors. Although she wanted to cry, she refused to give him the satisfaction.

"How did you find me?" she asked, stalling for time.

"You were easy to trace, darling. Remember, I'm the computer whiz."

"I didn't use any credit cards."

"You used your debit card, you stupid bitch! It's as traceable as a credit card. It was only a matter of time, baby. I must say this EMP thing did put a crimp in my plans though," Kyle sneered. "Oh, and I did want to save those last two paintings to burn in front of you, so you really get the message this time." He picked up *Dome Snow* and gazed at it. "I actually like this one, but you can't keep it."

"I won't let you hurt me anymore, Kyle." Adele did the one thing she knew would irritate Kyle the most. She turned her back on him and walked out the door.

He flung the painting at the woodstove, where it landed on the floor. "*COME BACK HERE!*" he screamed at her and lunged for the door.

Once outside, Adele ran. Her legs were shaky with fear and she was tired from a day of physical work. Kyle caught up to her quickly in spite of his injured knee. She threw his hand off of her arm and ran in the other direction.

"Stop it, Adele, or I'll shoot you with your own gun," he laughed. "I might anyway." He raised the pistol in her direction. Jeff tackled him from behind and the gun fired, the shot going high and wide off into the thin line of trees behind them. The gun flew from Kyle's hand as he and Jeff struggled. Adele leaped toward the gun and picked it up before Kyle's fingers made contact.

The rumble started low and vibrated through the ground. Adele looked around, confused. The noise and the vibration kept building. Jeff looked past her at the mountain, his eyes going wide.

"*Avalanche! Run!*" Jeff shouted, while Kyle struggled to stand. Jeff grabbed Adele by the wrist and pulled her back toward the dome.

Kyle started to run down the road, away from the building roar, realizing too late he couldn't outrun what was coming. He stopped, faced toward his ex-wife, and stood there defiantly.

Adele paused at the opened door and looked back in time to see a white wall of snow and ice sweep Kyle away. Jeff pulled her inside and slammed the door, locking it.

The concrete dome shuddered and groaned under the onslaught of tons of snow. It held fast as they were quickly plunged into darkness with the snow covering the windows, covering *them*.

It was a minor snow slide and was over quickly.

"Are you okay, Adele? Who was that?" Jeff held her close, unable to see in the dark that surrounded them.

She nodded, and then realized he couldn't see her. "I'm okay, I think."

"Who was that?" he repeated.

"Kyle Polez, my ex-husband. I don't know how he got out of the hospital or how he found me. I don't think I've ever been more frightened in my life!" She shuddered into Jeff's chest.

"I think it's safe to say he won't be bothering you anymore." Jeff pushed her back slightly, trying to see her face. He tightened his embrace when he felt her start to shake. "It's okay, Adele," he murmured into her hair. "Do you think he really would have killed you?"

"Oh, yes, no doubt in my mind. When I came here it was to hide, yes, but it was also to finish healing the broken bones. I broke my leg when he pushed me down the stairs, and he broke my arm after I divorced him. He is violent and crazy."

Jeff held her tighter. When she stopped shaking, Adele stepped back from him. "I'll find the kerosene lamp." She moved away from him, feeling the edges of the counter to guide her. A few moments later, she struck a match and lit the lamp she had purposely left on the stove so she knew where it was. The flame cast a brilliant, comforting light in the pitch dark room.

"Ah, that's better," Jeff said, taking the lamp from Adele to find a more central place, and set it on the art table. He stared at the pile of shredded art work, and looked over at Adele.

"Yeah, Kyle did that. He hated that I did something other people enjoyed and admired me for," she said. "He almost burned *Dome Snow*." Her voice faltered. "That's when I walked out. I knew he would rather physically hurt me than just emotionally hurt me, and that he would follow." She walked over to the woodstove and picked the painting up off the floor.

"You put yourself in danger to save that painting?" Jeff asked quietly.

"I couldn't let him destroy it, Jeff! It's not only one of the finest pieces I've ever done, it's also *yours*," she said. A realization seemed to wash over her and she started shaking again. "Do you think he's really dead?"

"I don't think anyone could survive that kind of crushing force, so, yes, I think he's dead." He picked up the pieces of the destroyed art. "What do you want to do with this?"

Adele walked to the table and looked down at the mess. "Each piece I do has a life; these are now dead and can't be resurrected. Burn them."

Jeff put them into the roaring fire.

Adele looked around the room as the reality of their situation occurred to her. "Jeff, how is it we weren't crushed?"

Jeff smiled proudly in the diffused light. "It's the design of the dome. It's meant to withstand tornado level winds and tons of snow. These have never truly been tested… until today. I'd say they passed the test admirably." He gave her a gentle hug. "At least *this* one did. I need to get outside and see what's happened to the others. I pray everyone was inside one of the domes!"

CHAPTER SEVENTEEN

Jeff unlocked the front door and cautiously opened it. Packed snow covered a third of the entrance. "We're in luck!"

Adele stared at the wall of snow blocking the door. "That's luck?"

"Of course it is. We aren't completely buried. I can get through the opening, get to the shovel in the carport, and finish digging us out. I hope. It will depend on how packed this is, which might be a lot," he said. "Even if I can't completely free up the doorway, we can still get out and get to the others."

"Do you think they're okay?"

"If they were inside, yes," he replied. "It will also depend on the angle of the snow slide. There may be areas completely unaffected."

"It's nearly dark, Jeff. Would it be safer to wait until the morning?"

"Yes, it would, you're right. I've got to know though, Adele," he said to her. "I'm going out to see if I can get on top and have a look around." He put his jacket back on and took the wooden desk chair to the door. He shoved the back legs into the hard snow for stability and climbed up. The top of the snow was now level with his knees.

"Wait!" Adele said. She hurried to the kitchen and brought back two large wooden spoons and handed them to Jeff. "Snow spikes." He smiled down at her and leaned out over the snow, thrust the wooden spoons into the mound and pulled himself out.

Once Jeff's feet disappeared over the mound of snow, Adele felt antsy and useless. She put another log on the fire; thankful she had refilled her inside supply. Her stomach rumbled and she glanced at her watch. It was nearing seven in the evening. No wonder it was so dark out, and no wonder she was hungry. She had pulled two steaks out of the silent freezer and set them on a plate in the equally silent refrigerator, hoping to keep a chill for the other food still there, especially her cheeses. Thinking back to her winters with her mother, she decided that a bowl full of snow would help too. Once the snow melted, she… *they*, could use it to wash or flush the toilet.

She got a large bowl from the cupboard, and made sure it would fit inside the refrigerator. When it didn't, she put it back and retrieved two slightly smaller ones that did fit.

Adele had left the door ajar, so Jeff could get back in easily. She opened it wider in time to hear him yelling. She stepped up on the chair to look out and saw him with snowshoes on and balanced on the packed snow. He was waving his arms and making hand-signals that she couldn't decipher, though his voice had a happy sound to it that sounded encouraging.

She chiseled some snow from the top and dropped it into the bowl on the floor. Picking at the hardened snow with a large spoon was taking a long time to get as much as she needed. Then she thought *what else do I have to do?* And she kept at it.

With the bowls full of snow and ice in the refrigerator, Adele lit a second oil lamp and used it to search her closet.

Jeff lowered himself carefully down to the chair and stepped off, pulling the two pair of snowshoes in with him. The place was bright.

"Where did you get those?" he asked, amazed at what he was seeing.

"My mother made me do it," Adele confessed, boiling water on the camp stove that balanced atop the useless electric stove. The wide room now had an oil lamp on her art table and a brilliant Coleman lantern on the work island.

"Remind me to thank her if I ever get the chance to meet her," Jeff said, admiring the propane fueled lantern.

The comment caused Adele to frown. "I hadn't thought about that, Jeff. I might never see or talk to my mother again. I should have thanked her when I had the chance for all she taught me." Her voice cracked.

"Hey, never say never." Jeff enfolded her in his arms. He tipped her face up and gently kissed her. "On a good note, I made limited contact with the others, enough to know they are all safe. The avalanche was semi-funneled between the condo-domes. The bad news is the office, restaurant, and, from what I could see, most of the hotel domes are buried. We will need to do a better inspection over the next few days. That means that most of the food is unreachable, unless we dig." He frowned at the implication. "Speaking of food, what are you cooking?"

"I was getting ready to steam some green beans, and pan-grill a couple of steaks." Adele smiled, trying to forget about her mother. "I know that considering the circumstances it might be an extravagance, but would you open a bottle of red wine for us? I know I sure could use a drink!" Her thoughts flicked back to Kyle for a moment and she shuddered.

"I didn't realize how hungry I was," Jeff said after finishing his dinner. "That was great, Adele. You mentioned about eating *your* food before taking any from the resort. Can I ask how much you have?"

"Keep in mind that I had plans right from the start to stay the winter. I enjoy cooking, Jeff, and I had intentions of keeping a low profile, for reasons you're now aware of, and so I stocked up." Adele thought again of her violent ex-husband now buried under tons of snow. She took Jeff by the hand and opened the freezer, then the refrigerator, and then each storage cupboard, one at a time.

Jeff was speechless.

"By my calculations, this would last me four or five months at the rate I normally eat," she smiled. "I can eat a lot," she said with a chuckle. "By rationing, I think this could last the two of us the same amount of time… but we might run out of wine."

"This has been an overwhelming day," Adele said.

"It certainly has," Jeff agreed. "I, for one, am really tired, especially after such a big meal."

"We skipped lunch, remember?"

Neither one wanted to approach the hovering situation.

"True. Umm, I can... uh, sleep on the couch, and keep the fire going," Jeff offered, somewhat embarrassed.

"Jeff, I meant it when I said that us being together was inevitable. I know I felt an attraction from the start. Didn't you?" She delicately stroked his cheek.

"Yeah, I have to admit I sure did," he replied, looking into her deep blue eyes; eyes made darker by the building desire they hid.

"Put a couple of logs on the fire. I'll turn out the lights. It will be much warmer if we share the bed."

CHAPTER EIGHTEEN

Jeff woke to something warm pressing against his back. He blinked a few times and remembered the pleasures of the previous night. He turned to find Adele's back snuggled against his, and he rolled over to hold her. Content, he drifted off to sleep again.

Adele roused to find Jeff's arms wrapped around her, and for the first time it didn't feel confining or suffocating. She stayed in that early morning pre-awake dreamy state for a few more minutes and then carefully slipped out of the warm bed. It was cold and dark; the darkness came from the dome windows being buried in snow, reminding her of their peril.

Adele restarted the fire and set some water to heat on the camp stove for coffee. She frowned, thinking she should have gotten the three burner model instead of the two burner, and then wondered how long the dozen small bottles of propane would last. Hindsight was always twenty-twenty.

Jeff shuffled out of the bedroom pulling on his shirt. He smiled when he saw Adele making coffee and hugged her from behind.

"About last night..."

"Yeah, it was pretty incredible, wasn't it?" she answered with a lopsided grin.

"It sure was."

She turned within the circle of his arms and kissed him.

"Careful," he grinned, "that could lead to something else and we have a lot to do today." Adele laughed and handed him a cup of coffee.

"What's first on the agenda?" she asked.

"I think getting into the offices. I need more clothes, these are going to start stinking soon," he wrinkled his nose. "And of course we need to get at the food. I don't know how much the guys were able to move yesterday."

"Jeff? Adele?" someone called out and pounded high on the door.

Jeff opened the steel clad door to find Aaron looking down at him. Behind him, Jeff could hear activity.

"Come on in," he said. "What's going on out there?"

"Matt and Chet are digging you out. Our dome only had the backside buried, thankfully, so getting in and out isn't a problem for us," Aaron said. "We thought we would get you freed so we could all work on getting back into the main structure."

"Hi, Aaron," Adele greeted him. "Have you guys had breakfast yet? I've got some frozen waffles I was going to fix for us."

"Chet made us pancakes this morning. He had packed a little bit of everything on the first sled and made it to the door as the avalanche hit."

"We'll have a quick bite to eat and join you in a couple of minutes," Jeff said.

Adele slogged gracefully in her snowshoes, with Jeff by her side.

"You've done this before," he stated, admiring the ease with which she walked over the crusty mounds.

"I told you, my mom lives in Upper Michigan and I spent many years there with her. At times, snowshoeing was the only means of getting around in the winter." They reached a section that seemed smoother than the rest, and began the descent, emerging on the hidden side of the other condo. Adele unbuckled her shoes and stuck them in the snow by the door, next to several other pairs. Jeff tapped on the door and opened it.

"Come on in by the fire," Beth said, from her place on the couch next to Aaron.

"Jeff, I wanted to ask you earlier if you have any idea how the avalanche started," Aaron questioned. "Or was it merely a loose snowpack?"

Jeff and Adele both relayed the arrival of Kyle, leaving out all the details concerning her art.

"He really was going to *kill* you?" Beth gasped.

Before either of them could answer, pounding started on the front door.

"Anyone in there? I need help!" Gwen Swanson screamed. They all rushed to see what the problem was. Jeff was secretly embarrassed he had forgotten about the last of his guests.

"What's wrong, Gwen?" he asked.

"It's Lane," she sobbed. "He won't wake up! I think he's... dead!"

The small group filtered into the private dome that the Swansons were staying in, and circled the couch where Lane lay peacefully.

Chet pressed his fingers to Lane's neck, and then picked up his hand, gently setting it back down quickly. "No pulse and his skin is cold already. I'd say he died several hours ago, in his sleep." He looked at a distraught Gwen, "When did you first notice he wasn't sleeping?"

"Only a short time ago," she whimpered. "I've been busy packing. Jeff, we were going to ask you to take us into town today. Lane said he wasn't feeling well and we thought it better to be near a doctor."

"Did he have any medical conditions?" Chet asked.

"He had a pacemaker. The battery was replaced two months ago, so that wasn't it," she answered. "Otherwise he was in good health, other than being near seventy."

Jeff and Aaron passed a knowing look between them.

"Gwen, this EMP we've been hit with, killed electronics. *All* electronics. It's a good chance that Lane's pacemaker wasn't working anymore," Jeff said as gently as he could.

"We should have gone sooner, with the others!" Gwen wailed.

"It wouldn't have mattered, Gwen." Adele put her hand on the crying woman's shoulder. "That pacemaker stopped on Thanksgiving night, at the same time our power went out."

After Beth had taken Gwen back to the communal condo for a cup of hot tea, the others had a conference.

"Now what?" Matt asked. "We can't just leave him here."

"Why not? It's cold and the body is protected. We can't bury him anyhow, not until spring," Jeff pointed out. "Gwen can't stay by herself though."

"She should move in with us," Chet offered. "That second bedroom is big enough to fit another twin bed." When Jeff raised his eyebrows, Chet said, "Look, I'm not suggesting anything kinky. Our unit is much more exposed then yours, Jeff, and we might need the extra security. Your place right now has only one way in, so it's easily defended."

"Defended? Do you think we're in danger up here?" Adele asked.

"We could be, that's all I'm saying." Chet took the blanket partially covering Lane Swanson and pulled it up over his face.

"Forgive me, Chet," Adele said, "you seem quite adept with this for a chef. Can I ask what your background is?"

"I was a medic in the Army for eight years," he sighed. "I took my college money and went to culinary school. I figured being a cook was less dangerous than being a paramedic." He looked around and laughed at the irony.

"We still need to deal with the food issue," Jeff said, bringing the discussion back to the plans of the day. "And that means getting into the hotel. Let's go."

Jeff, Adele, Matt, Aaron, and Chet, donned their snowshoes and took shovels to look for a way into the buried domes. Jeff walked ahead, stopping occasionally to look around or back, trying to orient where the hotel domes were.

"Why are we looking for the hotel domes, Jeff? I thought we needed the restaurant," Adele asked.

"The hotel portion was furthest from the snow slide so will have less for us to dig through. And since they are all connected, we get into one, we get into all."

Matt had ventured ahead and around. "Hey, Jeff!" he called out. "Come and look at this. We might have caught a break."

When Jeff reached the area Matt was standing, he turned a slow circle and stopped when a glint of something shiny caught his attention. He inched closer, being careful of the loose snow under his feet.

"Stay back, Matt, in case this lets go," Jeff ordered. He climbed the slope upward to the reflection and brushed at it with his heavily gloved hand, exposing a cracked window. "Excellent! Matt, call the others down here." Jeff used his shovel to carefully scrape away more and more snow. With the others now shoveling too, soon they had a four-foot section cleared.

"I suppose we could break the window to get in, but I'd rather not do that. It would leave everything exposed to the elements," Jeff said. "This is the northwest wing, which means the exit door is to the right three more feet," he pointed.

It took two hours of continuous digging to completely uncover the exterior door of the thick, hard packed snow and ice. Chet was the first to try opening the dented door.

"It's locked," he snorted. "We may have to break that window anyway."

Jeff reached into his parka pocket and produced a bundle of keys, selecting the master key that fit all the exterior doors.

The group stepped into the room that was lit only by the muted daylight from the window.

"It sure is dark in here, and it's bound to be even darker the deeper we go," Aaron said, stating the obvious.

Jeff looked at Adele.

"I'll go get it," she said, handing him her flashlight and heading back to their shared condo.

"Until Adele comes back with a bigger light, I think we should check these units for damage. As the snow melts, we'll have to board up anything broken to keep out the weather and critters."

"Well, crap," Chet said after venturing toward the main body of the hotel. "We might as well forget any other damage until we can clear this mess." The men gathered around the first fire door.

"Yeah," Jeff said, looking at the mound of snow that had pushed the door in and filled the hallway. "Let's grab our shovels, guys."

Adele kicked off her snowshoes next to the front door and pushed her way into the gloom. "Damn, this cooled off quick," she said to herself. She put several pieces of wood in the woodstove and left the door slightly ajar to give the dwindling fire a kick-start.

In her bedroom, she fumbled in the dark until she located the other working flashlight. In the closet was the lantern that Jeff would want. Although Adele was sure he was referring to the kerosene lamps she had, she knew he would prefer this one. She put an extra bottle of propane in a knapsack along with a box of matches and the lantern, thinking two bottles of fuel should be enough for now.

Passing the bathroom she lamented not having her morning shower, and thought of a solution. In the kitchen, she got out the largest cooking pot, added a bottle of water, and then filled it with snow. She set it on the woodstove to warm and closed the stove doors for a slow burn. Outside, Adele slipped into her snowshoes again, pulled the knapsack onto her shoulders, and set out for the buried hotel.

Matt and Aaron were taking their hand at digging, piling the snow in the hallway temporarily. The main objective was to get enough snow out of the way to close the door and make the hallway passable. The going was slow, with barely enough light coming from the one window and open door to see by.

Adele stepped into the room and out of the increasing wind. After removing the useless table lamp, she set the fifteen-inch tall lantern on the nightstand and made sure the propane bottle was tight. Jeff walked into the room as she was striking a match. The lantern blazed brightly and she adjusted the fuel flow for a steady bright glow.

"I thought you were bringing one of those kerosene lamps back," Jeff said smiling at her.

"This is much more practical for what we have to do. Come on, let's get this taken care of."

"Good lord, girl, where did you get that?" Aaron said with obvious delight when they stepped into the dark hallway.

"Blame my mother," she replied.

The group wandered down the quiet hotel with Jeff leading the way with the lantern. At the entrance to the restaurant, Chet came forward.

"I want to remind everyone that because of the power outage, I couldn't do my usual clean up."

"Don't worry about it Chet," Jeff reassured him. "What is going on now is new to all of us." He pushed open the doors to the cavernous room. The light from the lantern seemed to diminish as it reached out to the far shadows in the corners.

"You said you have lots of candles," Adele said to Jeff. "Maybe we should set some up on the tables so we're not bumping into things. That's something I can do while you four are loading up what you need to."

Matt set a large box on the nearest table and began unloading candles and holders. "Hey, there are even a couple boxes of eight-hour emergency candles."

Adele kept herself busy setting up taper candles on a few of the tables, and then took two boxes of the eight hour candles and a pile of saucers and left the room.

It took them an hour to fill three of the serving carts with perishable food and water, sorting things as they went. When the four men wheeled the carts out into the hall, they were surprised to find the area lit enough to see where they were going. Every ten feet there was a saucer on the floor with a long-lasting candle to show the way back to their exit.

"Adele?" Jeff called out, concerned until he heard her answer.

"I see you found my contribution," she grinned, stepping into the dark hall.

"This is ingenious," Aaron commented. "Manual emergency floor lighting."

"While you guys were busy, I went to get the sled," Adele added. "Too bad there's only one. Unless Jeff has got another one hidden somewhere?"

"Not that I recall," Aaron answered. "However, we have skis and plastic totes: I can make more sleds. In fact, it might be easier on us with smaller loads." He looked to Jeff with the question in his dark eyes.

"Go to it, my man!" Jeff answered, and Aaron took off down the hall in the opposite direction, commandeering Adele's working flashlight.

They pushed and rolled the three heavy carts into the access room, where Adele had left the sled.

"If we fill the sled and try to pull it up that slope, someone is going to have a heart attack and I don't want it to be me," Chet said, crossing his arms.

"Why don't we anchor the sled at the top, and form a 'bucket brigade,' handing one box up at a time? There are enough of us it should work," Matt suggested.

Jeff grinned. "I've got the best crew ever. Let's see how much we can move in one sled." Within fifteen minutes, the sled was filled with water, and Adele looped the rope around her trim waist and trudged off toward the first dome. The guys continued to hand up the boxes, making a stockpile for when the sled came back.

"That was quick," Jeff said when Adele returned.

"I unloaded and told the girls it was their job to get it in the house. I figure the faster the turnaround we have, the sooner we're done. Besides, everyone needs to be doing something."

It took most of the remaining day to move all of the water to the first dome, with a sled full going to Adele and Jeff's place. A few more hours and the fresh produce had been dealt with too by using the two new sleds Aaron made.

"I say we have a celebration tonight," Jeff announced. "Chet what can you cook up for this hungry and deserving crew?"

He looked over the meats that had made it in the last load. "How does chicken marsala on linguini with asparagus and a salad sound? We'll have to use up the fresh stuff first, like the lettuce and vegetables, so there's as little waste as possible."

"You won't get any complaints from me," Adele said, relishing the thought of fresh salads.

"I think we should bring back one more load... of wine," Jeff grinned.

"Good thing we didn't blow out those candles yet," Matt said.

"The last person out should do that," Adele reminded them. "And the first person in relights them."

Jeff took Adele's larger flashlight, gave her a quick kiss, and went out the door, dragging one of the sleds behind him to retrieve some wine for their celebration.

"Jeff seems to be taking an awfully long time," Adele said, pacing. "I'm going to look for him. Aaron, can I have my small flashlight back please?"

"Better yet, why don't I go with you?"

Inside the access room, they found a candle still burning, and rushed past the empty sled into the hallway.

"Jeff?" Adele called out. They were met with silence. "I think you should lead, Aaron; you know your way around here better than I do."

They arrived at the junction where the hotel room corridor met with the restaurant and were faced with a wall of snow.

Aaron aimed the flashlight at the walls and ceiling. Another window had given way and let in a drift of the icy cold snow. He handed Adele the light and started digging with his hands.

"I'm going to bring some of the lit candles here so we can both dig." The anxiety of knowing Jeff was trapped on the other side gave Adele renewed stamina and she hurried down the hall to collect the emergency candles.

Five bright candles lined either side of the hall when she was done. She pulled on her warm gloves and started pulling at the hard packed snow.

"I can see a faint light at the top on the right, which has to mean there's less snow there," Aaron proclaimed. "If we concentrate our efforts in that area, we should be able to get a tunnel to the other side quicker."

"This is going too slow!" Adele stepped down from the mound of snow they had made and dashed into the nearest room, returning with two wastebaskets. They both began scooping snow and slush, tossing it to the side.

"Jeff?" she called out again, climbing to the edge of panic.

"Hello? Is someone there?" they heard Jeff's faint voice and started digging with renewed vigor.

With a narrow passage three feet long, Adele stepped up and wiggled her way in. Another foot of scraping with the wastebasket and pushing the snow behind her, Adele broke through to the other side. She belly-slid down the other half of the window cave-in and landed at Jeff's feet.

"I'm so glad to see you." He hugged her tight.

"What happened?" Adele clung to him. "Besides the obvious."

"Nothing was out of the ordinary, the *new* ordinary, when I got here. I selected a case of wine and loaded a cart along with some booze, in case that's a preference for some," Jeff told her. "I heard a faint rumble and when I got here... so who else is on the other side?"

"Aaron," Adele said.

"Only Aaron?" Jeff was dismayed and a bit disappointed.

"No one knows there was another cave in or likely they would *all* be here digging," she assured him. "Let's get out of here. We can open the hall tomorrow."

"We're not leaving this behind, babe, not after all this," Jeff insisted.

She climbed up the icy slope and called out. "Aaron! He's okay. I'm pushing a box your way." With the first box out of her way, Adele wiggled back to the other side and Aaron pulled her the rest of the way out.

With Adele safely on her feet, Aaron took hold of the remaining box Jeff had pushed through and dragged it out. When Jeff saw Aaron reaching down the shaft, he took hold with both his hands and Aaron pulled him to safety.

"Whew! That's one narrow tunnel you two dug, and thank you." Jeff gave Aaron a hug and then kissed Adele deeply. "Let's get out of here, I'm starving." He limped down the hall.

"Jeff, why are you limping?" Adele asked, concerned.

"That's part of why it took me so long. When I was behind the bar collecting the liquor, I slipped on something and twisted my ankle," he said. "I think a can of something burst and the liquid froze on the floor. I hate to say this but it really hurts. You two are going to be the ones carrying everything since I can barely walk."

With Adele and Aaron carrying the boxes, Jeff scooped up the candles as they made their way down the hall, blowing each one out and then left them in the access room to be used the next time.

"You get lost in the dark, Jeff?" Chet teased. The three relayed what they had done and what had happened as quickly as possible. Chet paled, knowing he would never have fit in that narrow escape passage.

"I don't know about the rest of you, but I sure could use a drink!" Aaron said with a shudder, poured a whiskey neat, and downed it.

"I also twisted my ankle pretty bad, Chet," Jeff said, chagrined. "Any suggestions?"

"Lucky for you one of the things I brought back on the first trip was our first aid kit. I'm sure there is something in there." He opened the large white plastic box with a red cross on it. "Basic stuff, in here is all. Band-Aids, gauze, tape, Neosporin, scissors, tweezers, Ibuprofen, peroxide, things like that. No drugs of any kind." Chet gently moved Jeff's foot in different directions to gauge the extent of the injury and then wound an elastic bandage around his ankle snuggly. "Luckily, it's not broken. However, it is badly sprained. You need to stay off it as much as possible, and ice it for the swelling."

"Thanks," Jeff said. "This also brings to mind that we should have some new rules. The first is no one ever goes anywhere alone, especially not into the hotel. Got it?"

"That was incredible, Chet," Beth said, leaning back in her chair.

"I can tell it was well received," he replied, looking into the empty pot. "I hope we can figure out a better way for me to cook, though. That small woodstove doesn't have enough surface for everything I normally use."

"I'll see what I can come up with," Aaron offered. "And now we need to get you two back home," he said to Jeff and Adele. He stood and grabbed his jacket, as did Matt. With Adele leading the way holding the bright lantern, Aaron and Matt half-carried Jeff across the snow along the now well worn path.

"Before you go back, I have something for you," Adele said after the two men had deposited their boss on the couch. She returned from her closet carrying a new, still in the box, kerosene lamp and a bottle of lamp oil. Even though she had purchased several at her mother's insistence, she knew they really only needed one for the room they were in. This new, extended family she had needed one, too.

"I hate the thought of crawling into bed feeling so grungy," Jeff said after the guys left.

"Ah, that reminds me: how would you like to wash up in some nice warm water?" Adele offered. His eyes lit up and he smiled.

She helped him into the bathroom after setting the oil lamp on the sink. While he sat on the toilet seat, she pulled down a couple of washcloths and a hand towel. "I'll be right back."

When she returned, she was carrying the pot from the stove she had been adding snow to all day. With the drain closed, she poured half of the water into the sink and added the washcloths.

Jeff removed his shirt and dropped it on the floor. The water was pleasantly warm and he sighed when she washed his back.

"I think I can do the rest," he said, taking the cloth from her and wiping down his neck, chest, and armpits with more warm water.

"And I know you want to ask," she laughed. "My mom always had a pot of water heating on her cookstove. She always said, *you never know when you might need hot water.* It's one of those lessons she taught me that I never think about anymore. Since we no longer have running water, I think it's a good thing to keep doing."

CHAPTER NINETEEN

"I know it's only been three days, Adele," Jeff complained. "I'm so used to being active this feels like three weeks!"

"Tired of my company already?" she teased him.

He caught her hand as she walked past. "I don't think that's possible. It's just that—"

"I know, Jeff. In fact, I thought it might be a good break to host a dinner party, with five of our closest friends," Adele said, chuckling, because right now all they had were five friends, and each other.

Aaron and his wife Beth arrived first, a reluctant and depressed Gwen trailing behind them. Matt came in carrying a couple of bottles of red wine, and Chet handled the large wooden salad bowl, per Adele's request.

"You don't look any worse for wear, boss-man," Aaron chided Jeff, who was still admonished to keep his foot iced and elevated.

"I've had a good nurse," Jeff said, "and she won't let me do jack-shit." Meanwhile, Chet was busy undoing the elastic bandage.

"She's done a good job. The swelling has gone done considerably," Chet informed him. "Another day or two and you can start walking around again. Please take it easy, boss, okay?"

"I got it, Chet."

"So what's for dinner, Adele?" Chet asked. "I'm anxious to try someone else's cooking."

"Grilled steaks, rice pilaf with mushrooms and peas, biscuits, and your salad, though I'm considering keeping the salad for myself," she answered with a mischievous grin. Chet cocked his head in surprise. "If you can pull all that off on that woodstove over there, you can have *my* job," he said, still uncertain she could do that.

"I don't want your job, Chet, I'm just happy with something to do and Jeff is happy with some company besides me. Right, dear?"

"Still, I hope you don't mind me taking notes." Chet handed her a glass of the ruby red wine Matt was pouring from the freshly opened bottle. He wandered over to the woodstove and lifted the lid from a deep pot, noticing it sat elevated on a metal trivet to prevent scorching. Inside was the rice and mushrooms waiting for the peas. A fry pan with a lid revealed biscuits ready for turning. "Jeff, this woman is a keeper. I'm impressed, Adele. I'm still wondering how you're going to grill the steaks." He lifted the lid on another large pot to find plain water.

"I'm hoping you'll help me with that," she answered. "What I did though, to collect enough snow to melt so we could wash, was dig out the grill that was buried on the deck." She pointed to the glass door. "I got tired of it being so dark in here during the day that I worked at exposing the window. Partway down, I discovered the grill. We got more light, we got more water, and we got the grill back."

"Jeff, if you don't want this woman, I'll take her," Chet said with a grin.

"If you try stealing her from me, I'll fire you," Jeff replied.

"Those steaks were perfect, Chet, thank you for doing that," Adele praised the chef.

"Everything was perfect. May I propose a toast?" Jeff stood, leaning on his good foot. "To eating well in spite of our problems."

"So what's been going on while we've been cooped up?" Adele asked the others.

"We've been back in the hotel, and cleared out the hallway again," Aaron said. "I wanted to check with you first, but I think we should board up the windows in the main hall. I know there are some sheets of plywood in my shop that would work. It would be better to have it dark than to get trapped again."

"Good idea. I think we're going to see a lot of shifting snow packs as the weather warms," Jeff replied. "Have you brought out any other supplies?"

Matt was standing by the windows, waiting to make a comment. "Um, Aaron, didn't you say a few days ago that you had some ideas for fixing the generator? That sure would make it easier on all of us."

"Yes I did, but I haven't had the time to really look into it, sorry. If I can borrow your lantern tomorrow, Adele, I'd like to check out my workshop. From a long view, I think it's completely buried, so there is no light in there at all," Aaron said.

"Of course," Adele replied. "There's only a couple bottles of fuel left though. If you can refill them somehow, that would really help."

Aaron laughed. "*That* project is a piece of cake."

Four men dressed in white camouflage insulated suits watched from a nearby hill in the early morning light. Two lay on their bellies with binoculars while the other two stood among the branches of a stately spruce tree, well hidden from view.

"What do you see, Walter?" Tanner asked. After their plane went down on Thanksgiving, killing the pilot and guide, Tanner had assumed leadership of the hunting party.

"There appears to be seven people; four men, three women. Though in heavy gear it's hard to be sure."

"Women?" Tanner smiled.

"Why don't we just go down there?" Walter asked.

"Are you stupid? No one in their right mind walks into a group of unknowns, especially if they're outnumbered," Tanner admonished him.

"Bill is getting worse. Maybe they have a doctor or know where we can take him. At the very least, maybe they know what's going on," Walter pleaded.

Tanner, former Black Ops, thought about what Walter said. "Maybe we should do that, Walter. We go in seeking help, recon the situation, and go from there. No one does anything without my say so."

Bill stepped out from the cover the tree gave him. A light sheen of fever-sweat glistened on his forehead. "Good, I don't think I can take another night out in the open."

The four men moved toward the compound slowly and in full view, Tanner and Carter in front, Walter following behind holding up a weak Bill. They stopped a hundred yards from the first occupied dome.

"Hello!" Tanner called out. "Anyone here?"

Jeff and Chet stepped out of the dome, surprised to hear a strange voice.

"Hello, there," Jeff replied, surprised at the arrival. "Where did you come from?"

"Our plane crashed last week. We've been on foot ever since. Can we come closer?" Carter asked, hoping to create trust.

"Sure." Jeff was put at ease by the polite distance and request. Adele had been watching the exchange from inside. She picked up Jeff's shotgun and joined them. Her handgun was snug in its holster tucked in the back of her faded jeans and covered by her new down jacket.

"Ma'am," Tanner acknowledged her presence when they were within a few feet, his eyes lingering on her pretty face. "One of our group was injured during the crash. We were hoping someone here could help or direct us to a doctor."

"Come inside and get warm and we'll take a look at him," Jeff offered.

"That's much appreciated, Mister...?"

"Atkins, Jeff Atkins. Adele, would you get the others?" he said with underlying meaning.

She handed Jeff the shotgun, looking squarely in his hazel eyes as if to say *be careful*. She slipped on her snowshoes and disappeared over what looked like a hill to the recent arrivals. It was easy for her to surmise that Jeff wanted everyone together in case this wasn't what it appeared to be.

Jeff led the four men to the dome entrance and helped with Bill when he stumbled. "You can leave your gear over there," he pointed. "Without water and power cleaning up in here is difficult, so we're careful about tracking stuff in."

The four men unzipped and removed their jackets and lowered the matching bibs to waist level. Walter helped Bill get his bulky white suit over his injured arm.

When Jeff saw the torn sleeve and the dried blood, he got Chet a bowl of warm water and a cloth to clean the wound. Since the clotted and drying blood had glued the material to Bill's skin, Chet first soaked the shirt and then peeled the sleeve back, revealing a long cut and a massive infection. At least that part of their story seemed true.

"What the hell happened?" Chet asked.

"When the plane went down we were tossed about quite a bit. Bill was impaled by a chunk of metal. How bad is it?" Walter asked.

"I won't lie," Chet said, pouring some peroxide on the wound, "it's bad." Bill passed out from the pain and Chet took the opportunity to probe. "The cut is really deep and septicemia has set in." He wrapped the arm in fresh bandages and faced Tanner, recognizing who was in charge. "I don't have any antibiotics. He needs a doctor or he's going to die."

"Where do we find a doctor?" Walter asked, even more worried about Bill.

"The town of Avon is about ten miles down the road. Even though it's only got a population of about a thousand, there's a good hospital there," Jeff answered.

"Would you mind if we rested a bit first?" Tanner asked, stalling while he sorted out the situation and the options in his head. "We've been on the move for days with little to eat or drink. I have to be honest: we're exhausted. We saw your smoke this morning and headed here. I don't know if we could make those ten miles without some rest first, and maybe something to eat—if you can spare it."

"Sure. Beth, can you get our guests a bowl of soup?" Jeff said over his shoulder, keeping an eye on the three men who insisted on standing in spite of their professed exhaustion.

After they finished a bowl of hot soup and guzzled a bottle of water each, everyone relaxed a bit. "Thank you, that really hit the spot," Tanner said, while Walter tried to coax Bill into having some soup. He thought it was a waste of food.

Matt, Aaron, and Adele came in, stomping the snow off their boots. Tanner's eyes instantly flashed with racism when he saw Aaron and he quickly tamped it down.

"Okay, Tanner, here's the rest of our crew. I know all of us want to hear what happened and why you were so far off the aviation path when the EMP hit," Jeff said.

"EMP? Is that what happened?"

"Apparently. Some guy in Avon heard a ham radio broadcast just before everything shut down. We were hit with three long range missiles, and if they took down the grid, they were armed with nuclear warheads," Jeff went on. "It fried everything electronic."

Tanner nodded thoughtfully. "That explains why we just fell out of the sky." He looked at the others. "We were on a fly-in hunting trip south of the Canadian border and on our way back. Our guide and the pilot were killed on impact, and we lost one other of our men from injuries a few hours after the crash. We stayed with the plane for another two days, waiting for a rescue that never came. That's when we decided to try hiking out. When we saw the smoke from your chimneys, we changed directions and came here." He looked around at the cozy room. "You've stumbled on a really nice set-up here, Jeff, and you're fortunate to have such lovely ladies for company." His eyes lingered on Adele again.

"No stumbling involved, Tanner. This is the Geo Dome Resort. *My* resort, and we all live here. Everyone here is an employee or a paid guest. We were closed for November for upgrades and were finishing Thanksgiving dinner when everything quit. The next night we were hit with an avalanche, which buried most of the units," Jeff explained, intentionally leaving out how the avalanche started. "And since you will be here for a day or so, let me introduce everyone." Jeff did some fast thinking, taking into account all of the body language he saw emanating from Tanner, especially the way he looked at Adele. "This is Aaron, my right arm and best friend. He's my can-do-everything handyman, and you've met Beth, his wife, head of the housekeeping department. Chet is the resort chef and former paramedic. To call Matt a waiter doesn't do him justice; he has many talents. Gwen is a guest. Her husband died shortly after the EMP when his pacemaker quit. And this is Adele," Jeff put his around her shoulders protectively, "my wife." Adele stiffened at that announcement and Jeff applied the slightest pressure to her arm to quell her surprise. "Now, why don't you gentlemen make yourselves comfortable, maybe take a nap if you need to. We have work to do. Matt, would you help Beth and Gwen bring in more wood? Chet, Aaron, Adele, you're with me. We need to finish up those repair projects."

Jeff grabbed the shotgun and they all moved quickly before Tanner could question what they were doing.

"What was that all about, Jeff?" Chet asked once they were out of earshot of the new arrivals.

"I don't trust Tanner. There is something hinky about him, and I sure don't like the way he was looking at the women," Jeff said. "Something feels wrong about the whole situation. Chet, do you think he's military?"

"No doubt in my mind, and from some elite group. Why did you leave out *my* military experience?"

"If he knows you've got military in your background, you would be one of the first he would disable, if it comes to that," Jeff explained. "Aaron, sorry, bud, but that man is a racist and he already hates you, especially for having a white wife. His mind could never understand how lucky Beth is to have you, and *that* may keep her safe from him." He turned to Adele. "Tanner is the alpha of his group. I'm the alpha of our group, and if he had any designs on you, he now knows you're taken and he'd have to go through me."

"I understand," she smiled at him. "We do outnumber them though."

"Yes and no," Chet commented. "We have more people and Bill is in no condition to be a concern, but the other three have high powered rifles and if they were on a hunting trip, they know how to use them. What do we have Jeff, a shotgun and a rifle? We're outgunned if it comes down to that."

"I have this," Adele said, removing her pistol from the holster at her back.

"Like I said before, Jeff, if you don't want her, I'll take her," Chet laughed and Jeff punched him in the arm. "How much ammo do you have for that?" he asked.

Adele smiled at the antics. "I have a brick back in my closet, plus two more magazines."

"So we've evened the odds a bit. Now what?"

"Now we wait and see if they cause any trouble," Jeff replied. "I think we should tone down the food resources, Chet. How about making something really bland and skimpy for dinner tonight? We don't want them knowing how much food is here. We might never get rid of them if they knew."

"Got it. I've always wondered how far I could stretch one can of soup and a bowl of rice," Chet chuckled.

"Aaron, how is the generator coming along?" Jeff asked.

"You really think I can concentrate on that when my wife is back there with that asshole?"

"No, of course not. Hey, where did we leave the rifle?" Jeff asked embarrassed that he didn't remember what he did with it.

"It's probably still under the front seat of your truck, boss-man."

"Okay, we've stalled out here for an hour. Chet, you get supplies for dinner. Aaron, take the shotgun and go back to help with whatever Matt is doing. Adele and I will get extra ammo for the rifle and shotgun from my office, and then the extra magazines for her gun. I don't want those guys knowing about the rifle. However, to make it available for any of us, I'll make sure it's loaded and leave it in the carport behind one of the shovels. Let's go."

"Well, that meal was interesting," Tanner said after dinner. "Being a restaurant, I would have thought you had more food on hand."

"Usually we do," Chet said casually. "We were closed down for the month of November for repairs *and* cleaning. The freezers and coolers were shut down for sanitizing. I had already ordered the restock for the winter season, so somewhere in the state is a truck load of *our* food." The lie came smoothly. "Don't pay that bill when it comes in, Jeff," he snorted.

"You didn't like the rice, Mr. Tanner? I thought the dish was rather innovative," Gwen said. "Please don't insult the chef, or these guys will make *me* cook, and then you'll be glad you left for town." Gwen had caught on real quick to what was going on, and played along with it like a pro.

"Well, it's getting late and I'm sure you guys want some sleep," Jeff said, standing. "Who has watch tonight?" he asked looking at Matt.

"I think it's my shift, boss," Matt replied. He got up from his chair and put another log on the fire and sat down again. Jeff exaggerated his limp and handed the shotgun to him.

"Why do you have a night watch?" Carter asked. "I thought this place was pretty safe."

"For the most part it is. Guard duty also means keeping the fire going. You needn't concern yourself with your safety or comfort for tonight." Jeff held out his hand to Adele.

"Goodnight, everyone," she said stifling a yawn. Outside, Jeff lost his limp and they hurried to their condo and out of the increasing wind.

CHAPTER TWENTY

Chet served pancakes for breakfast, made from a box mix, with plain water and no syrup. He still had syrup, lots of it, and lots of powdered milk too. Jeff said to make the meals simple and bland and that's exactly what he planned to do.

"That was good, Chet, thank you," Gwen said. "I still miss syrup, though. Are there any maple trees around here that we can tap in the spring?"

"I'm not sure, Gwen. That's something to ask Jeff, though don't hold your breath. All I see are evergreens and more evergreens," Chet answered, setting a few more thin pancakes on the now empty serving plate.

"I will say those were hot and filling," Tanner said, putting his plate in the sink of warm soapy water. He moved over to stand by the windows and gazed out at the lightly falling snow. "Don't Jeff and Adele join you for meals?"

"Usually," Aaron answered. "Rarely for breakfast though. They're still honeymooning." Beth playfully slapped his shoulder and he pulled her into a quick hug and a brief kiss.

Tanner turned away, disgust written on his face. His thoughts went to Adele. Beautiful, quiet, and blonde. He had a thing for blondes.

"Tanner, Bill is worse. He's burning up and I can't wake him," Walter said. "We've got to leave *now* and get to town."

Tanner hovered over the unconscious Bill. He pulled out his handgun and shot Bill in the forehead. "There, now you don't have to worry about him and now we're in no rush to leave." The room went deathly quiet.

Walter grabbed Tanner's arm. "Why did you do that? We could have saved him, you coldhearted son of a bitch!" Tanner backhanded him and he slumped to the floor, his gray head rested on Bill's unmoving chest.

"Hey, man, what are you doing?" Aaron angrily stepped up to Tanner and got in his face.

"Back off, *boy*," Tanner growled, raising the gun again. Carter picked up his rifle in support. Beth pulled on Aaron's arm, moving him away. Walter wept.

Gwen ignored Tanner and knelt beside Walter, placing her hand on his shoulder in comfort. "He was your friend, wasn't he?" she asked quietly.

Walter shook his head. "He was my brother!"

Everyone looked at Tanner at that statement and backed away.

"Yes, he was your brother, so what? He was dying and you know it. I put him out of his—and our—misery." He looked down at the oldest member of his group and shook his head in pity. "Get a grip, Walter. He never would have survived the trip anyhow."

"Was that a gunshot?" Jeff stood, alarm lacing his voice. He and Adele had just finished a breakfast of hash browns and eggs when the report filtered through the walls.

"Sounded like it to me," Adele said. "We better check."

"You stay here," Jeff said. "Please. We need at least one armed person on our side *not* over there. Let me find out what's going on first." He slipped on his boots, wincing at the pressure on his ankle, pulled on a hooded jacket, and was out the door before she could protest.

Adele quickly changed from her morning attire of sweats to jeans, a sweater, and a vest to hide the gun she added, and then she waited.

Jeff grabbed the loaded rifle from the carport and burst through the front door of the large dome. "What's going on? We heard a shot." He took in the scene quickly: Tanner and Carter had guns focused on everyone in the room; Gwen was kneeling beside Walter, who was softly weeping beside Bill.

"That bastard killed Walter's brother. Shot him in the head so they wouldn't have to take care of him." Chet's voice was low and dangerous.

Jeff spun around and glared at Tanner, his knuckles going white as he gripped the rifle stock. "Have you no respect for anyone, Tanner?"

"Respect? Now that's an interesting concept," he replied dryly.

"Yeah, you ought to try it sometime," Jeff said with contempt.

"Drop the rifle, Mr. Atkins." Tanner's voice was soft, low, and mean.

"And if I don't?"

"Then I'll shoot you. Your choice."

Jeff lowered the rifle and set it on kitchen island.

"That's better," Tanner said. "Now that all this is out in the open, I don't have to be someone I'm not. I was getting *real* tired of playing nice. Now, I think I'll go pay your lovely wife a little visit." Jeff lunged at him, but Tanner was quicker. He swung the gun and caught Jeff alongside the head, sending him to the floor. "Carter, keep an eye on everyone. If they misbehave, shoot 'em." He shrugged on his jacket and was out the door before Jeff regained consciousness.

Because of the angle of the domes and the height of the snow, Adele didn't see Tanner cut across the snow covered yards. She was washing dishes when the door opened.

"Jeff?" she called out.

"Not quite," Tanner answered. She spun around to face him.

"What are you doing here?" Her voice was strained but steady.

"That should be obvious by now, little lady. I've come for some fun." His eyes gleamed with a madness Adele recognized, one she had seen in Kyle many times.

"Fun? If that means sex, never! You're a pig. You smell bad, and you're disgusting." She laced her voice with all the contempt she felt.

Tanner reached out and backhanded her across the face, sending a trickle of blood oozing from the corner of her mouth. She stumbled and backed up to the work island. The memory of Jeff's gentleness washed over her and comforted her, and the memory of Kyle's abuse hardened her resolve. She only stared at him, saying nothing.

"Oh, I think you liked that, didn't you? You like a bit of roughness, is that it? Or maybe a *lot* of roughness? Yeah, I'm gonna have me some real fun now." He turned away from her, readying another punch. He didn't want to hurt her too much; he wanted her awake and aware, crying and pleading when he took her. The thought excited him even more.

His fist was in mid-swing when he caught sight of the 9mm pointed at him, and he laughed, momentarily dropping his hand.

"That is unexpected, but you don't have the guts to shoot me," he said, taking a step closer.

Adele pulled the trigger, blasting a hole in his chest from four feet away.

Chet applied a cold wet towel to Jeff's face, wiping up the blood welling from the gash on his temple.

Walter stood and faced Carter. "What are you doing, John? Tanner is crazy, we both know that. You don't have to do what he tells you, not any more. Be reasonable, these are good people." Walter pulled his sidearm and aimed it at Carter. "What would your wife think if she saw you like this?"

"It doesn't matter anymore, does it, Walter? We're never going to see our families again. They are safe at home in Florida and we're stuck here in this godforsaken corner of Montana, likely forever." His voice was shaking now. "All because... because of..."

"Go ahead and say it John: All because of Tanner!" Walter yelled at him. "He was the one who wanted this damn hunting trip! You served with him, *you* should have known he was nuts, yet you, yes *you*, talked me and my brother into coming. And now Billy is dead, and that nut job is over there doing God knows what to that nice lady. It's as much your fault as it is his."

While Walter had Carter distracted, Matt rushed him. Carter saw the movement and reflexively pulled the trigger, sending Matt flying backward, where he collapsed against the wall like a ragdoll. Walter then shot John Carter, his cousin.

"I didn't want to do that," Walter choked out. He looked to the others staring at him when they all heard the gunshot from the other unit. "Here," he set his gun down on the table, "someone go save her from that animal!"

Aaron grabbed the pistol and ran out the door, leaving his jacket behind. Halfway across the snow mound, he met Adele coming toward him. When she saw him she collapsed to her knees.

"Adele, are you hurt?" he asked.

She shook her head. "I shot him. He was going to rape me and I shot him," she sobbed. "Where's Jeff? I need to see Jeff." Aaron helped her to her feet and took her back to the group.

Jeff was coming around when Adele and Aaron opened the door. The carnage was worse than she imagined. She dropped to her knees beside Jeff, crying, and hugged him.

"Oh, Matt." Jeff lifted Matt's head and cradled it, gasping for breath as the tears flowed. Adele knelt beside him, offering what comfort she could.

They dragged Tanner's body out of Adele's condo and left it in the woods, minus the heavy snowsuit that one of them could use. Matt, Carter, and Bill were laid out in a row next to Lane Swanson and the doors locked, until spring would let them dig appropriate graves. Beth and Gwen washed the blood from both units. It was a solemn night for everyone.

"That was an incredibly brave thing to do, Adele," Jeff said, holding her tightly in the dark.

"I had no choice. I could not, *would* not, let him touch me!" She involuntarily shuddered.

"Try not to think about him. He's gone, thanks to your quick thinking. Let's try to get some rest. I have a feeling that tomorrow is going to be another busy day."

They lay in bed, cuddled in the warmth of several blankets and each other.

"Have you noticed how quiet it is now?" Jeff murmured into her hair. "There is no refrigerator humming, no clocks ticking, no ambient white noise that says the power is on. Now we can hear what's under all that."

"What *is* under all that?"

"The sound of darkness," he answered.

"Hmm, I think I've had enough darkness in my life to last me forever," Adele sighed. "Do you think this will ever end?"

"I don't know, why?"

"I think about all the money I've saved over the years to enjoy 'later,' and now it seems that 'later' has arrived and it's all gone, for good," she answered wistfully. "And you know, I don't miss it."

"If you think *you've* lost money, you have no idea," he said flatly.

"What do you mean, Jeff?"

"Did you ever wonder how I could afford to build all of this?" he asked.

"I've wondered, but it's not my place to ask."

"I won the lottery."

"Really?"

"Five hundred million dollars," he replied in the dark, wishing he could see her response. "I took the payments and after taxes I get twelve million dollars every year for twenty years. Well, I *used* to." He laughed. "You know what I can do with twelve million dollars a year? Anything I want... like build my dream resort."

"And here I was worried about a measly few million."

CHAPTER TWENTY-ONE

Sheriff Claude Burns slumped in his wooden office chair, which creaked with his bulk. At fifty years old, his hairline was receding rapidly and his once fit waistline was competing just as quickly. "Is this what is going to keep happening?" he asked aloud. "Refugees seeking shelter and help when I can't even help the people already here?"

"If that question was directed at me, Sheriff, the answer is: likely." Allison McCarthy set a fresh mug of coffee in front of him. Allison had been his secretary for the last ten years, ever since he was elected to office. Two years after his wife passed from cancer five years ago, Allison also became his sometime lover. They maintained separate homes out of decorum, and spent one night a week together.

"What do you think I should be doing about that?" he asked, looking at her, wrapped in an oversized sweater and wearing fingerless gloves.

"First, we need to get more wood in here to burn," she said with a shiver. "Next should be a conference with Mayor Hawkins."

"Henry? Yeah, I guess you're right. He's the elected official that's supposed to run this town."

"The next thing is I think you should move in with me. I've got that woodstove you had Mike Miller install last year, and he's kept me supplied with plenty of wood. You can't sleep here to stay warm," Allison said, crossing her arms over her ample chest.

He sighed. "You're right again, Al. I'll bring some things over tonight." He got up from his chair and walked to the door. "If you see Mike, flag him down and ask for a load of wood for here. And tell him I need to talk with him, okay? I'll go to the Wilderness Outfitters and talk with Henry."

"Good afternoon, Claude," Henry said. "I was wondering when you would be stopping by." He sat down in the rocker by the woodstove. "We've got quite a mess on our hands, don't we?"

"You could say that," Claude sat in the other chair and was quiet.

"What is on your mind that we do?"

"As mayor of our fair town, that's really up to you, Henry. I'm only the enforcer."

"I have a feeling something has crossed your mind though."

"We're already getting people coming in from outside, wanting to be taken care of—and fed." Claude stood to pace.

"It's only been two days. Are the residents running out of food already?" This astonished Henry. The town of Avon was so far off the beaten path that most everyone kept a well-stocked pantry. That was, until Walstroms came to town and made it easy to buy groceries a couple of times a week.

"I don't think so, but it might not be too much longer, and I think we ought to get ready for that. When it happens, it ain't gonna be pretty," Claude said.

Henry stood. "Then as mayor, I say we call a town meeting and discuss getting into Walstroms and taking what we need."

"Can you do that?"

"Sheriff, who is going to stop us? From all indications most, if not all, of the country is in the same situation. I say we act now, before someone else raids the place." Henry laced his fingers together in thought. "I see our biggest issue is getting food from Walstroms to the people without running vehicles. It's a long walk for some."

"We also need a plan for a systematic distribution. We can't have a free for all, Henry."

"Agreed. Sit a bit, Claude, and let's talk this out," Henry suggested. "What needs to be done first? And would you get me that pad of paper behind the counter and a pen? These old bones don't like the cold."

"Getting the people together would be first," Claude said.

"Not really. Shouldn't we find a way into the store first and see the condition? We know there isn't any power for lights."

"Without power the coolers have shut down. There is food that will spoil and fairly quick: meat, produce, everything in the freezers too." The sheriff stood and looked out the windows. "I bet in the camping section there are some lanterns we could use. I know I've got an old kerosene lamp somewhere that I should take to the office. There might be more of those too. People get weird if it's too dark." He picked up another log to put on the fire. "Henry, why don't you lock up and come down to the station? Allison has the place warmed up, coffee on the stove, and I think she could help us plan things out."

Henry chuckled. "Before we go, Claude, take a look around."

The sheriff looked around the store and stopped. "It would have bit me, right?"

"Right. The lanterns are in aisle four, but I don't stock fuel, too hazardous." Henry picked up the Maglite flashlight that was on the floor next to the rocker and flicked it on, sending a fine beam that cut through the dark interior. "Most of the flashlights are LED and aren't working for some reason; however, I've got a box full of those shake and break light sticks that are better than nothing."

"What about food?" Claude asked, now understanding that the Wilderness Outfitters was a treasure trove.

"Dried foods are best saved for when the fresh stuff runs out. Energy bars, jerky, things like that are all shelf stable. With winter approaching I already got in new inventory on gloves, hats. and boots." Mentioning the clothes instantly made Henry think of Ms. Michaels and that clod looking for her. "Claude, if someone were planning on spending the winter here, where would they stay?"

"There are several resorts around here, Henry, you know that. The Geo Dome would be at the top of my list though. And that reminds me, Jeff was just in town dropping off some of his guests and he was driving his truck!" Claude exclaimed. "I wonder if he would loan it to us for a few days."

"Must be an old truck to have survived the EMP blast."

Sheriff Burns and Mayor Hawkins each carried a box of supplies, walking down Main Street toward the town offices. Out front, was a wagon full of split wood pulled by two Belgian draft horses.

"Mike, it's good to see you." The mayor shook the young man's hand. "How are you holding up with this calamity?"

"I'm doing fine, Mr. Mayor. Not being dependent on the grid has its advantages," Mike Miller said. "Sheriff, Mrs. McCarthy said you needed wood. I put some next to the woodstove. Where would you like the rest?"

"If you would help me move a desk, you can put it in one of the offices. I doubt they're going to be used anytime soon," Claude replied. "As for payment, I could write you a chit, but we both know it wouldn't be any good. So, young man, what can we barter?"

Mike smiled. "Let me think about it. I've got all I need to survive, except maybe smokes. Bad habit I know, but it's my only one."

Henry noticed Mike's tattered gloves. "Mike, may I suggest some new gloves for you as payment?"

The young man looked down at his hands. "That would be perfect, sir."

"Sheriff, I'll be back in twenty minutes." Henry left to retrieve two new pairs of gloves from his store.

"These are really nice, Mr. Mayor," Mike said, admiring his new wool-lined leather work gloves. "Thank you. I think I'm going to like this barter thing."

"About taking me up to the Geo Domes, Mike, how soon could you do that?" the sheriff asked.

"I still have another load of wood to deliver to Mrs. McCarthy and then the horses need rest. How about tomorrow? Would that be soon enough?"

"Thank you. That would be fine."

"I promised him a hot dinner in payment for the wood," Allison said after Mike drove off with the horses to replenish the wagon. "Which brings up my next question. Henry, Claude, would you care to join me for dinner? I'm making a pot roast."

"I'd be delighted, Allison," Henry said. "May I ask how are you cooking? I thought everyone was on all electric."

"I think I'm one of the few who have a gas stove, which can be lit with a match," she boasted. "That reminds me, Claude. If you don't need me here, I'd like to go home and get dinner started and be there when the wood shows up."

"What that woman of yours said has me thinking," Henry said when they were alone again.

"*My* woman?"

Henry laughed. "Come on, Claude, the whole town knows you two spend a lot of after work hours together."

"Nosey people," Claude harrumphed, sending Henry chuckling into his mayoral office.

"Come on, Romeo, we need to make some lists."

"What was it Allison said that has you thinking and about what?" Claude asked, settling into the comfortable green leather chair in front of the mayor's wide oak desk.

"Her stove. Even if we get enough food out of Walstroms, how are people going to cook? Few enough of them even have heat." Henry pulled a steno pad from the top drawer and took a pen from the cup that sat on the far right corner of his desk. The cup had a picture of his granddaughter laminated on it. She had perished along with his wife and daughter in a head-on collision twenty years earlier and he still missed all of them.

"I guess we should check out the camping section of Walstroms for portable stoves. Who do we give them to though?"

Two days after the EMP, The Gold Mine bar reopened for business. The owner, Jonas Johnson, who claimed to be a direct descendent of the legendary, and possibly mythical, Jeremiah Johnson, spent those days fixing all the mining lamps he had collected.

Deputy Tighe Teagan pushed the heavy wooden door open and stepped into the muted light. "Are you really opening, Jonas?"

"You bet I am. Never let a good disaster go to waste," the bald and portly man laughed. "It didn't take nearly as much time or effort to get all these old oil lamps working again, and with light I've got customers." He came around from behind the bar and put another chunk of wood into the old pot-belly stove. "New cover charge is one piece of firewood. I'll make an exception for our law enforcement. You want a drink, Tighe?"

"No thanks, I'm on duty. I might be back later, though." Deputy Teagan looked around his favorite haunt. There were times he needed to get away from his wife and girls and be with the guys and this was where he went. "Here I thought all those old lamps were only decorations to add ambiance." He noticed nearly a dozen old oil lamps hanging on hooks from the ceiling and a few on tables. The glow was a welcoming sight.

"They were, until the power went out. Same for that old pot-belly," Jonas said. "Tell me, Tighe, do you think the lights will be back on soon?" At fifty years old, Jonas looked over sixty, and knew his drinking, bad diet, and hard life had taken its toll on him. He picked up the large antique teakettle from the stove and took it behind the bar. Pouring some of the warmed water into the closed sink, he dampened a well-used cloth and began wiping down the wooden bar.

"I don't think so, Jonas. Not according to the few reports the sheriff has gotten in. We are all going to have a lot of adjusting to do."

"Obviously the power is out, and I know cars don't work for some reason, but what else is affected? Wait, didn't I see that Jeff Atkins from the fancy resort up Hog Back, driving a truck yesterday?"

"Yeah, it's a really old truck that doesn't have any electronics in it. That's the problem with everything, Jonas. The electronics, and if you think about it, about everything has some kind of circuit in it. Computers, cash registers, cellphones, even land lines. I think that's what concerns me the most: no communications at all and that includes any news from outside the town itself. We might all revert to having a kid around to run messages." Deputy Teagan slumped on a barstool.

"What if there's an emergency?" Jonas asked.

Deputy Teagan had no answer.

"Come on in, guys!" Jonas greeted his first customers.

"Hey, Jonas. Man, am I happy to see you open," Clyde said. "I saw the sign out front and had to go back home for some firewood." The others behind him set their chunks of wood down next to the old cast iron stove.

Jonas knew his customers. He lined up three chilled beers on the bar.

"How are you keeping the beer cold without electricity?"

"It's winter! I packed a tub with snow and filled it with bottles and cans. We all have to adjust somehow," Jonas laughed, wiping the moisture rings with a cloth again.

It wasn't long and the bar was packed as usual. And it wasn't long before the men were drunk and rowdy. Someone clapped another on the shoulder in friendship a little too hard and he fell into another, who pushed back. The fight sparked a mental dismissal of the new surroundings, and an oil lamp crashed to the floor, spreading liquid fire across the exit.

The fire alarm never sounded.

CHAPTER TWENTY-TWO

Claude was stunned at the news of the fire. There were no alarms, no fire trucks blaring, and no phone calls to alert him.

"How many did we lose, Tighe?"

"We won't know for sure, Sheriff, until it cools down more. My guess is nearly fifty. The place was packed when I left, just before it all started. I suppose the only good news is that since The Gold Mine was on a corner, there was only one nearby building and it was only scorched."

"It hadn't occurred to me that we are now without a fire department." Claude sat staring out the window while the deputy silently left.

"I heard the news, Claude," Henry said. "What are we going to do about all the bodies? The hospital morgue can't handle that many."

The sheriff sighed. "I know it's going to sound rather gruesome, but there's an old house on the outskirts of town. I say we put any and

136

all deceased in there for the winter, and when it warms in the spring, we torch it. Instead of a mass grave, we'll have a mass cremation."

"You think there will be more?"

"This is only the beginning, Henry. Only the beginning."

Precisely at noon, Mike Miller pulled his team of horses up to the town offices.

"Meant to tell you, Mike, these are beautiful horses," Sheriff Burns said after he climbed into the wagon. When he ran his hand down the nearest one's flank, the horse softly nickered, obviously accustomed to the attention.

"Shh! They'll hear you and forget they're supposed to *work*," Mike said, half seriously. "Have you been up Hog Back since the power went down?"

"No, but Jeff Atkins has been here twice in that old pickup of his. Last time was two days ago and we haven't had but a dusting of snow since them so it should be open," Claude said. "How are you managing out on your farm without power?"

"Only thing I miss is the satellite TV, but I'm getting more work done without it. Oh, and the refrigerator, though with it cold out I leave stuff on the enclosed porch and it's fine," he replied. "I'm not real dependent on the power. How about you?"

"I'm okay, I guess. I fear for the town though, in all honesty. Not everyone is as independent as you are, Mike, so you be careful if people start showing up at your door."

The horses plodded along, steady and strong though not very fast, which was all right with the sheriff. It had been too long since he'd taken some time off to enjoy life in the Rockies. The air was cold and clean and refreshed his spirit.

"The horses are never in a hurry, are they?" Claude commented, shifting on the hard wooden seat.

"They can be if I ask them to, I'm the one who isn't in a big hurry, I'm rather enjoying this," Mike replied. "We can make the time up going back. Even with the wagon empty, it's still weight on them and we're going uphill. I don't want to exhaust them. Coming back they'll be quicker going downhill." Mike was quiet for a few minutes. "Sure is pretty up here, isn't it? So quiet, too."

The sheriff nodded, listening to the crunch of the hard snow under the wagon wheels. One of the horses snorted, and then a pileated woodpecker took to the air sounding its strange cry. A black squirrel scampered up a barren deciduous tree and chattered at the passing wagon.

"Do you venture up here often, Mike?"

"Usually only in the fall when I volunteer to take the schoolchildren on a hayride," he said. "Riding around town sitting on the straw doesn't excite the young ones like getting into the woods does. And then there's the teenagers." He grinned at the memory. "We leave at dusk for an hour. I tell ya though: *those* kids mess up the straw bales real good in that short time!"

The ten mile trek took them forty-five minutes.

"Whoa!" Mike called to his team. "What's that up ahead?" He tied the reins loosely around a rail and jumped down into the calf deep snow.

Claude walked toward the drift of snow across the road. As he got closer he saw it wasn't a drift at all.

"Looks like a small avalanche. It's not too packed and it's still settling." He stepped as close as possible to check the signs, much as an animal tracker would. "This happened late yesterday or perhaps during the night. I'm fairly confident Jeff had already made it back to the resort. I tell ya, no one is going up or coming down for quite a while. See how far to the west it goes, will ya, Mike? I'll check the east side."

They gingerly followed the ragged outer edge of the deep snow into the woods. Mike returned to the horses a few minutes before Claude did, and began turning them around.

"You have a shovel or something I can dig with? There's something odd about fifty yards from here," Claude said.

While Mike finished getting the team set in the downhill direction, Claude called out, "Mike! Give me a hand here. It looks like someone is trapped in the snow!" They dug rapidly for another ten minutes before the person was uncovered enough to drag free.

Mike touched his fingers to the man's cold throat. "There's a pulse, Sheriff. Faint, but it's there." He carefully looked at the unconscious man. "I wonder what he was doing out here. Those boots wouldn't keep anyone's feet warm *or* dry."

"No gloves either, though they could have come off when he was swept away from wherever he was," Claude surmised. "At least he had a reasonable hood on that parka, likely saved his life."

"Let's get him into the wagon." They covered the unmoving man with horse blankets and began the long journey back.

"I don't know what the doctors at the hospital are going to do with him without power, but we need to get this guy there as soon as we can," Claude said, glancing back at the mound of blankets.

Mike snapped the reins and sent the horses into a downhill trot.

One week earlier, it would have been a strange sight to see a horse drawn wagon pull under the emergency room portico, and Sheriff Claude Burns would have been the first one to move them along. A lot could happen in a week.

Claude jumped down from the rough seat that had brutalized his back and butt for the past half hour and dashed into the dark ER.

"I need a gurney!" he shouted at the nurse behind the check in counter.

"We aren't taking in any patients, Sheriff," she said.

"You're taking this one. Where is Dr. Sam?" He grabbed the icy cold rail of the nearest gurney and rushed back to the doors. Without thinking, he ran headlong into the glass doors, expecting them to open, and bloodied his nose when they didn't. "Crap," he said, pushing the panic-bar of the side door and pulled the stretcher behind him.

Mike had already removed all the heavy horse blankets that covered the stranger and dragged him to the tailgate of the old wagon. Mike and Claude gently lifted the still-unconscious man and laid him on the gurney. They pushed the wheeled stretcher to the wide doors, where Nurse Ellen Tibbs had manually opened them.

Dr. Sam Cory was waiting for them inside, having heard the commotion and yelling.

"What happened to him, Claude?" Dr. Sam asked.

"We found him buried in a small avalanche up Hog Back Road. By the look of the snow pack, he's been buried for twenty-four hours, maybe longer."

"That might have saved him. Take him into the first exam room where I've got a lantern and let me have a look, though I don't know how much I can do for him," Dr. Sam said, shaking his head.

"Thanks, Mike," Claude said. "Can you hang around for a bit? I might need you and your wagon again."

"Yes, sir, Sheriff."

Between the doctor, nurse, and sheriff, they managed to strip the wet clothes off the stranger and wrap him in several blankets trying to warm his body up.

Sheriff Burns removed the wallet from the back pocket of the man's jeans and opened to the license. "His name is Kyle Polez, from Texas. Yet another stranger in town." He dropped the wallet on the side table.

CHAPTER TWENTY-THREE

"What do you think, Sam? Is he going to make it?" Sheriff Burns asked the doctor hovering over the still unconscious Kyle Polez.

"He's young and healthy, and being buried in the snow helped to insulate him. So yes, I think he's going to make it," Dr. Sam said. "That's the good news. The bad news is he's suffering from dehydration and hypothermia and his hands are badly frostbitten. It will be touch and go for a few days, but there's a chance one or both will have to be amputated. At the very least several fingers," the doctor reported. "And how I'm going to do that is the next problem."

"What do you mean?"

Dr. Sam leaned his shoulder against the doorjamb and sighed. "Claude, it's been hell in here ever since the power went down. Fortunately, with it being a holiday weekend, there were no surgeries scheduled, and being a small facility the place was more than half empty. However, we were also running on a skeleton crew since it was Thanksgiving. Most of our staff lives someplace else and can't get here now." He took a deep breath and stared at the dark ceiling fixtures. "In the first twenty-four hours, I lost ten patients. *Ten!* All those were on some type of life support and died quietly, thank goodness. Old Mable needs oxygen for her asthma and is struggling for every breath now. She won't last much longer. There are five more patients that I'm trying to send home, but three of them don't have anyone to go home *to*. And it's so cold in here, everyone is constantly complaining."

"What about this guy?" Claude asked, bringing the doctor back to the current problem.

Sam straightened up and looked at his longtime friend. "How am I supposed to operate without adequate lighting? And I mean *literally* operate. That lantern over there is barely enough light for me to see by and not bash my shins on something."

"How long before you will know if you have to… amputate? Maybe we can come up with something," Claude offered.

"We've got a few days, but that's all. As his body warms and his blood circulates, I'll be able to tell where and how much tissue has frozen beyond repair."

Sheriff Burns and Mike Miller walked into the town offices to find Allison setting out sandwiches for lunch.

"That sure looks good, Ms. McCarthy," Mike said.

"Help yourself, Mike. Claude, Henry is waiting for you in his office."

"I'm glad you hung around, Henry, saves me from tracking you down to tell you about our next problem," Claude said, sitting in the blue leather chair. He told the mayor what they found near the resort.

"A stranger from Texas?" Henry asked thoughtfully. "Dark brown hair in a buzz cut?"

"Yeah. Do you know him?"

"No, but he was in my store several days ago. Not a nice person, Claude. Best to keep an eye on him."

"He's not going anywhere for a while," Claude replied. "Let's get back to business. Since we can't get to Jeff to borrow his truck, I've asked Mike Miller to hang around. I suggest you and I get up to Walstroms and check things out before the town meeting in the morning. At least we'll have an idea what we're up against."

Using a crowbar, the sheriff and Mike pried the heavy glass doors apart at the Walstroms superstore. After propping the doors open, the three men stepped into the gloom and switched on their flashlights.

"We have two objectives right now. The first will be to find the camping and hardware section and see if there are any lanterns or anything else that can be used for light. The next will be to check out the food section for the condition of the coolers and freezers," Mayor Hawkins announced. "We should each take a basket in the event we find something useful."

They cautiously headed up the main aisle and veered off to the left midway. Mike stopped as they cut across the store and tossed a few things in his basket.

Claude nodded in silence when he saw the dozen boxes of candles Mike had selected.

"Uh oh," Henry said coming to a stop beside a display. "Someone has already been here. Look." Some shelves had been striped clean, while others had been pushed over, items thrown to the floor. "Let's make this quick, guys."

Claude led the way further in, his service weapon drawn, and arrived at the ammo counter. "Shit." The locked glass cases had been smashed open and all the ammunition was gone. "Whoever it was knew what they were going for. Thankfully Walstroms carried only a few rifles and no handguns," he said, staring at the broken gun case. "There are still shotgun shells left. We better take them before whoever it was comes back." Mike added those to his grocery cart.

"Next aisle over is the outdoor stuff. Let's hope there's something left."

The trio slowly edged around the end-cap, expecting the worst.

"We're in luck, if you want to call it that. Henry, I'll hand you these stoves and lanterns. Mike, take all those bottles of lamp oil and those small bottles of propane, would you?" Claude was busy pulling items off the shelf and didn't hear the footsteps approaching until too late.

"Hold it right there," a voice commanded. "Oh, it's you, Sheriff. What are you doing?"

"Geez, Alvin, you about scared me half to death! What are you doing in here?" Claude said, recognizing the middle aged man.

"I'm the store manager, remember? Even though you're the sheriff, you're still stealing," Alvin Alpo said, lowering his rifle. "I'm responsible for this stuff until the power comes back on or until the night manager shows up from Butte."

"Alvin, don't you know what's going on? The power isn't coming back for a long time, if at all," Henry said. "Also, we noticed the hunting section has been ransacked. When did that happen?"

"Late last night a bunch of guys broke in through the back. They must have been after ammo only because they left after cleaning me out. I'm not stupid, Sheriff, I hid until they were gone."

"Well, we'll help you board up where they broke in, and I'll have a couple of deputies rotate guarding the place. The town needs what's in here, Alvin, plain and simple, and if the entire state isn't under martial law, we are as of right now."

"I'm okay with that, Sheriff, now that I know what's going on. How can I help?"

"Can we assume that the food department is still intact, Alvin?" Henry asked.

"Yes, Mr. Mayor. As cold as it's been, most things are still okay. In fact, the only things that are suffering right now are the freezers. If you're looking to feed the town, sir, I'd suggest a pizza party. That stuff is starting to thaw."

"Is there anything in here that is or could be a manual heater?" Claude asked. "The hospital is getting desperate."

"There are three kerosene heaters in the aisle next to paint. I don't have fuel though," Alvin said.

"Henry, you and Mike take those two full carts back to the front and get two more. We'll meet you in the food department," Claude said.

"Where have you been staying, Alvin? Are you sleeping here?" Claude asked, pushing his cart as he followed the store manager through the various aisles.

"I thought it a good idea, Sheriff. I've got an office overlooking the store above the Service Center." He looked at Claude, then looked at his feet. "Truth be told, I'm glad you came along. This is too much of a responsibility and burden for one man. When the power went out I was glad I had given everyone the holiday off. Being here alone, though, is kind of spooky." He handed Claude boxes holding the bulky heaters.

"I'm glad we ran into you too, Alvin. Knowing your way around is going to make this a lot easier for us. Come on, let's grab two more empty carts."

They met up with Henry and Mike in the produce section where Mike was loading a cart with lettuce.

"Some of that is already going bad, Mike," Alvin said.

"I know, but my horses don't care. I've been working them hard all day, they need to be fed and watered. Besides, you don't want it rotting in here, do you?"

Alvin grimaced. "Let me help you."

An hour later, they had twelve shopping carts lined up in the entrance filled with lamps, lanterns, candles, produce, and stacks of pizzas.

"Now the question is, how are we going to get these carts into the wagon?" Claude thought out loud. Mike calmly dropped the back gate on the truck and slid a thick sheet of plywood out and down, creating a ramp.

The first stop the wagon made was at the hospital where they dropped off two propane lanterns, a heater, one camp stove, and several pizzas, with the sheriff promising to bring some kerosene back as soon as they unloaded the rest.

"Where are we going to take the food, Sheriff?"

"For now, back to the town hall. We'll pass out the pizzas at the meeting in the morning. After that, we need to find someplace that can cook mass amounts with what fuel we have available," Claude answered. "Oh, and here's a down payment for your help, Mike." He handed the young man two cartons of cigarettes.

"Thanks, Sheriff. I would help out just to help out, though," Mike said.

"I know you would, Mike. I also want you to know we appreciate what you're doing for us."

CHAPTER TWENTY-FOUR

"Quiet down, everyone!" Henry yelled to be heard above the din of voices. He pounded the gavel yet again from his position at the podium. Four other councilmen sat two on either side of him.

Claude and Allison had come in early and set up chairs and the new kerosene space heater in the large and seldom-used meeting room. The chill was barely off when the first resident arrived and took a seat at the front. Before long, the room was filled to capacity, the extra bodies helping to raise the warmth. All the unwashed bodies also added a slightly unpleasant odor to the air. Allison remedied that by spritzing a room freshener above the space heater, hoping the rising heat would circulate the flowery scent.

"Thank you. Now, we've got a lot to cover this morning, so please, let us speak and then I'll open the floor to questions. Obviously we have a crisis on our hands of great magnitude. It would appear that the country, and that's *country*, not *county*, has been hit with what is called an EMP, an electromagnetic pulse. With limited information before everything went down, we suspect it was likely caused by a high altitude nuclear missile."

The crowd burst into shouts and questions. Henry pounded his gavel again.

"Please, everyone, quiet down! Thank you. Now, we don't know who is responsible or even if for certain that was it, although it has the signs of it according to some of our more learned residents. That being said, the power isn't coming back on anytime soon, if ever, so we will need to make some adjustments.

"A number of you heat with wood; you're the lucky ones. If you have friends or relatives that don't, be kind and invite them in.

"Some of you have a means to cook while others were dependent on their electric stoves. We're open to suggestions on how to handle these situations. Yes, Father McMahon?" Henry said when the priest stood.

"The church will open its doors to everyone in need. Our kitchen facilities might be limited, however we do have gas stoves and ovens. What we don't have is food to cook." The priest sat down.

"Thank you, Father, and we can help with that," Sheriff Burns said from his spot to the right of the council table. "Yesterday, I officially declared martial law in Avon." The crowd murmured again. "A few of us were in Walstroms and it is now under the jurisdiction of... me. The day manager, Alvin Alpo, is giving us his full cooperation to take whatever is needed. Right now we have approximately two hundred pizzas waiting to be heated, which we will deliver to the church after this meeting or to those who want to take theirs home. I'm asking that everyone self-ration your food to make it last as long as possible."

"We will make more food available as we can get it out of there and into a location for distribution," Henry said. "Now, do we have any questions?"

"What about water? My tap isn't working."

"Good question. We will distribute all the bottled water available. After that we'll figure out a means to haul water up from the Mountain Cap River. Plus we all need to collect snow to melt for flushing. By the way, your faucets don't work because the city well needs power for the pumps, so no power means no water."

"Martial law, which I've no doubt is in force all around the country right now, generally means confiscation of all firearms," Claude said. "That ain't gonna happen in this town. Every one of you with a weapon may need it to protect yourself and your loved ones, just don't get stupid."

"What about school?" Alex Peters called out from the crowd.

"All schools are suspended until further notice," Henry answered.

"What if we want to leave?"

"Then leave, Alex. Where are you going and how are you going to get there?" Claude said. Alex sat back down.

"What about my medications?" someone else called out.

"That's something you need to take up with Dr. Cory. I will warn you, he's got his hands full right now."

Mae Collins stood. "What do we do if someone... dies?"

"Then you contact me and I or one of my deputies will deal with it, Mae," Claude said softly. "Do you need to talk to me?"

"Not yet. My dad was too weak to come to the meeting, and his heart meds are about to run out, so I'm concerned, is all," she answered and sat down.

"This also brings up the matter of the pharmacy at Walstroms. All of their stock will be moved to the hospital and will be under the supervision of the doctor," Henry stated. "Moving pharmaceuticals to the hospital is twofold. The first is, of course, the doctor that is still here will know best how to distribute what we have since the pharmacist lives in Butte and I doubt can get here. The second reason is there has already been a break-in at Walstroms. This also ties in with Sheriff Burns wanting all of you being able to defend yourselves. The break-in was for ammo. Everything that was there is now gone. The next break-in might be for drugs, and we want what is left under guard and safe for when Dr. Cory needs to use it."

"I think that all went well, considering," Henry said to the sheriff.

"Yeah, considering everyone is still in shock and aren't hungry yet. Eventually both of those controls will end, and then what?"

"I don't know, Claude, I don't know," Henry said. "I'm going out on a limb here and ask that you and Allison take me in," he laughed. "That sounds really strange to me. Oh, and I think we should move all the ammo I have at the Outfitters here, maybe locked in a cell, along with the few firearms. The dried foods too. I want to make that place as unappealing for a break in as possible."

CHAPTER TWENTY-FIVE

"How is your patient doing, Doc?" Claude asked.

"His body temperature is back to normal now, although he still hasn't regained consciousness," Dr. Cory answered. "And thanks for that heater, it's helped. We've managed to move all the remaining patients down here to the ER where the heater is and have shut off the remaining rooms to help conserve that heat."

"That's good. I'm going to shut the heater off for a short time, take it outside and refill it for you." When he was done, Claude returned it to the ER waiting room and relit it, sending billows of hot air out to quench the chill.

"So what's your opinion on the frostbite, Doc?" Claude asked.

"While it might be a bit early to say for sure, it looks like he will lose a couple of toes on each foot, two fingers on his left hand, and most, if not all of the fingers on his right hand. I'm going to say he was damn lucky you two came along when you did. Another twenty-four hours and he would have been dead."

"I wonder how lucky he's going to feel when he gets the news."

"My oath is to keep him alive, Claude. If he doesn't wake in the next forty-eight hours, I will perform the surgery and he will have to deal with it. I don't know what this man did for a living before, but I hope it didn't involve his hands."

"What the hell is this?" Cal, the guy in the black balaclava, asked over his shoulder. "I thought you said it was easy to get into this place!" The thick plywood now covering the back door at Walstroms was attached with construction screws making access impossible.

"It was easy the last time I was here," Gene replied. Not even out of his teens, he kept tugging his green winter face covering out of his eyes. The full ski mask didn't fit his smaller head well and kept slipping. "With all the noise the other guys made while trashing the place, someone obviously heard." He jutted his invisible chin out, knowing he was one of the perpetrators the other night that made all the noise and was why he was ousted from the new gang.

"Well find us another way in, bucko, or your ass is grass." Fred, a big guy with a hunter orange balaclava, said, giving Gene a shove.

"Only other way in that I know of is the main doors around front," the kid said, walking away. He was thankful for the mask so the other two couldn't see his fear.

"Now what?" the big guy snarled. "There's a light on in there; it's coming from a lantern sitting on a chair, which means someone is here and guarding the place. Damn!" The three slunk around the corner letting the night hide them.

"If we wait until the time is perfect, we will never get in there for the drugs in the pharmacy," Cal said.

"Then let's do it." Fred pulled a large wicked looking knife from his boot and gave the door a harsh shove.

"Who's in here?" came a strong voice from the dark.

"We didn't think anyone would be here," Cal spoke up, leading the trio in the deception. "We were hoping to find some food. Is there any left?"

A middle aged man carrying a shotgun stepped out from the shadows. "Since the mayor is giving away this food, I guess it would be okay for you to take some."

Fred's long legs took him close to the guard in three steps. "Thanks," he said, shoving the knife into the startled man's midsection and slicing up. He pulled the knife free as the guard collapsed to the floor, and then wiped it on the man's jacket. "Let's find that pharmacy." He picked up the dropped shotgun and flashlight and quickly moved away.

Gene stood frozen, shocked at the uncalled-for violence.

"Come on, little stock boy, we need you to show us the way," Cal roughly grabbed Gene's arm and pulled him past the inert body and into the bowels of the Walstroms store.

"What the...?" Fred faced Cal. "It's already been stripped clean!" Had there been enough light to see by, the other two would have seen the rage building in the big guy's face.

"So where is it?" Cal twisted Gene's arm to an unnatural angle.

"How should I know?" Gene whimpered. "These shelves were full a couple of days ago!"

"Liar," Fred snarled, and drove the still-bloody knife into the boy.

CHAPTER TWENTY-SIX

"How's the generator work coming along, Aaron?" Jeff asked, sitting down at their table for a cup of coffee. He and Adele had already eaten at her—*their*—place. Jeff was still getting used to the arrangements, overwhelmed that someone so beautiful and talented would want him.

"Better than I thought it would. Well, maybe not better, but definitely quicker than I hoped. Of course, there were other things that had priority, like draining the pipes in all the units," Aaron answered. Jeff raised his eyebrows. "Hey, boss-man, you said that came first."

"Yes, I did, didn't I? So what are you doing and what can any of us do to help?" Jeff asked, stirring a teaspoon of powdered milk into his cup to cut the bitter brew.

Aaron stood and looked out the window at the snowy landscape. "Again, I'm not sure if this will work, so I don't want everyone to get their hopes up, okay? We need to pull all the batteries from every car we can get to, and take them to the generator dome. I've got a lot of rewiring to do, so someone will need to pick up on my chores."

"Wiring?" echoed Walt, who kept to himself and was quiet most of the time. "I'm an electrical engineer. Is there anything I can do?"

Aaron stopped pacing and smiled at the new member of their group. "Oh, yeah, you can help. It would make it much easier on me to not have to explain ohms and amps and voltage to a second pair of hands. Jeff, do I have your permission to take the batteries?"

"Sure, Aaron, anything you need, although wouldn't the batteries have fried in the EMP?"

"Not necessarily. They're only batteries, and don't have any electronics or chips in them, they just need something to get the power that's in them out and usable."

"The batteries are heavy. I don't think we should put more than two in a sled," Jeff told Adele. He took the necessary tools out of the old pickup truck that was stuck in the avalanche snowbank and disconnected the battery in Adele's Tahoe, then disconnected his own. Each of them cradled a battery out to the sloped area that had been created by foot traffic and set them in one of Aaron's makeshift sleds. Beth took the first load and headed toward the generator dome. Gwen silently followed the duo to retrieve what they needed from her car and then to the Bentley left behind by the Jenkins'.

Once the sled was full, she looped the tow rope around her waist and followed the smooth tracks left by the other sled, meeting Beth halfway.

"If you follow my tracks, Gwen, you can't miss the place. Where are Jeff and Adele headed next?" Beth asked.

"Over to the Bjork dome and then I think back to Aaron since there aren't any more cars out on this side."

"Here are five batteries, Aaron. Will that be enough?" Jeff asked.

"We should have a minimum of eight. We still have a couple of cars and my pickup in the resort garage," Aaron answered, with a hint in his voice.

"Yes, sir, boss-man," Jeff replied, a chuckle lacing his deep voice. He and Adele left for the garage that sheltered employee cars and other work vehicles.

Adele peered inside the dark, cavernous building and waited for Jeff to manually lift the huge doors to let in some daylight. Inside was Matt's Subaru, Beth and Aaron's Jeep, the resort's new pickup, and the two old vehicles Jeff was restoring.

"No wonder I never saw anyone's cars. You kept them hidden," Adele said.

"Not hidden, only out of sight. I didn't want the place to look like a parking lot. There are five available batteries here. We'll leave the two older cars alone for now and see if this is enough for Aaron. Besides, I'll need one for the truck when the snow melts." Jeff lifted each one out and handed it to Adele, who lined the three up by the door.

"Can you explain what you're trying to do, Aaron?" Jeff asked after they set the rest of the batteries next to the others.

"I'll try. Remember when we first wired the condos I suggested we wire every unit with a separate switch in the breaker box? That was so I could disconnect one for repairs without interrupting the others," Aaron said.

"Right, and we did the condos first to lay the underground wiring before we were even open so it wouldn't disrupt anyone," Jeff remarked.

"Yes, and when we added the hotel part, we continued with each having their own breakers, likewise the offices and the restaurant." Aaron walked over to the massive number of circuit breakers, all neatly labeled, and pulled the main to each box. "Everything is now completely disconnected from the generator, which really doesn't matter since it's fried anyway. However, the power *to* the generator is still there, it just can't get in."

"What are you saying, Aaron?" Jeff had a cautious optimism in his voice.

"The windmills don't have any electronics and are still functioning, and fortunately were missed by the avalanche. That's where the batteries come in. I think we can rewire the turbines to charge the batteries directly, hook up the inverter to limited circuits, and give the two domes, the well, and maybe, *maybe* the restaurant, at least the lights."

"Wouldn't the inverter have been destroyed too?" Adele asked.

"Yes, and this one was," Aaron said, tapping the huge powerhouse, "but not our spare."

"Spare?" Jeff said. "I didn't know we had a spare."

"Honestly, I had forgotten about it. When we went from the six domes and office, to the domes, the hotel, and restaurant, the inverter we had wasn't adequate. So I ordered a new, bigger one, and put the first one away in my tool chest—my metal tool chest—which acted like a Faraday Cage. I was looking for some tools when I found it."

"Aaron," Walt chimed in, "if it was in a metal case without protection, it might still be fried. Unless… was it in something else first?"

"When I was storing it, I wrapped it in bubble wrap to protect it from getting banged around." Aaron grinned in the dim light. "I think what we should test out first are the lights for in here so Walt and I can see what we're doing."

"Aaron," Jeff said slowly, "if this works, I'm giving you a raise, a *big* raise."

"*If* it works?"

"What the hell, even if it doesn't work, I'd give you a raise for giving us all some hope. When will you know?"

"Come back in an hour."

Inside their dome, Jeff paced like an expectant father.

"Jeff, why don't you do something useful, like help me haul in wood?" Adele said, stepping in front of him to halt his motion.

"If this works, Adele, we won't need to burn wood anymore. We'll have power back and with power we have the electric heat," he replied, overjoyed at the thought.

She dumped her armload on the floor next to the stove. "What if it doesn't? Besides, even if it does work, and I sure hope it does, we might not be able to use everything we used to."

"What do you mean?"

"The times my mother used the generator, and it was a good sized one, she always reminded me to be conservative. Any appliance that generated heat drew way more power than anything else. That included the dryer, stove, refrigerator, water heater, and furnace. When one was on, the others couldn't be without risk of damaging the generator.

"She always told me to prioritize, and water came first, which meant the well. Second was lights," she said. "Water is the only thing critical we don't have enough of that we haven't already adapted to. Lights don't draw a great deal of power if you remember to shut them off when you leave a room."

Jeff looked at her and sighed. "Okay, so we can't use everything. What would be *your* priority?"

"The water heater," she replied without hesitation. "I really miss hot showers. And the water heater will suck up a lot of juice because it stays on all the time."

"Can we turn it on and off? Maybe dial it back?"

"That's something to ask Aaron, which," she glanced at her Cinderella watch, "it's been an hour."

Jeff and Adele, Chet, Beth, and Gwen waited while Walter and Aaron systematically flipped individual switches to the off position. With a nod from Aaron, Walter pushed the main breaker to the on position. Nothing happened.

"Aaron…" Jeff said.

"Patience, boss-man," Aaron replied. He looked at the breaker boxes, spotted the one he wanted, and pushed it to the on position. When the overhead lights came on, everyone cheered. "Everyone, this was the test run. We don't have everything rewired yet. All we did was hook up one of the newer batteries to the inverter; one that

I was pretty sure still had at least a partial charge. Now what we do, since we have lights," he grinned widely, "is wire the rest of the batteries to link with each other and into the windmills. That will take time; I'm guessing the rest of the day. And then the batteries need to charge, which shouldn't take much since they aren't completely drained. Tomorrow we should all have lights!"

Chet hung back while everyone else filed out. "Aaron, could you turn on the lights in the kitchen for maybe an hour? I want to get some things for a celebration tomorrow night."

"No problem, my man," he went to the bank of circuit breakers and flipped one to the on position. "Let me know when you're done. This battery isn't being charged. Lights don't draw too much, but they still draw."

Chet took one of the few flashlights that worked and made his way down the dark halls toward the kitchen. When he entered the restaurant dining room, he could see lights on behind the swinging doors that led to his domain. His heart pumped faster and he almost wept for joy. Knowing his time was limited and not wanting to press his luck, he pushed the roll cart into the big doors that opened silently.

From the freezer he pulled out several chickens, a whole tenderloin, and a bag of shrimp, testing each item for how frozen it was. He was pleased. Another week and everything would be too thawed to use. For now, because he had insisted on keeping the doors closed even when he was inside, most everything had stayed partially frozen. This was something most people didn't realize: solidly frozen food would *stay* frozen for a long time inside a highly insulated cooler if not exposed to warmer air. With the weather below freezing, and no heat in that dome, the food was staying good longer than he'd expected it to. The fresh produce, on the other hand, was gone. As much as they had eaten over the past two weeks, some had gone to rot.

Chet put everything on the rolling cart, along with a few of his favorite knives and his sharpening stone. He added a large bag of flour and some yeast to make bread once he could use the stove, two bread pans, and more of his favorite condiments. On his way out, he stopped at a plain door that concealed the wine cellar. He selected three bottles of their best champagne.

"That was quick," Aaron said when Chet stopped in. "What are we having for dinner?"

"Tonight is chicken," Chet said while Aaron shut the breakers down to the kitchen. "Tomorrow is a surprise." He thought a moment after Aaron went back to his wiring. "When you finish, will there be enough power for the freezers?"

"I can't answer that, sorry. I won't know until things are up and running and we can test the output. With only two domes running instead of six and the office, I hope so." Chet's face fell. "There are too many variables, Chet." Aaron said gently. "I'm going to talk with Jeff about a rotating schedule that will let us have most everything back, just not at the same time."

"Here comes the real test," Aaron announced. Everyone was gathered in the generator dome for the momentous occasion.

Although it had been only a few weeks without power, it felt like an eternity to most. "Last night, after we wired the seven batteries together, I adapted the windmills to charge them. And before you ask, Jeff, I left the one battery off so we could still have lights in here. This morning, that one was disconnected from the inverter and added to the bank, giving us a full eight batteries. It's a bit low, but will charge quickly now."

"At that point, we wired them to the inverter, which was already wired to the circuit breakers," Walt said, prideful that he had contributed something important to this group that had saved his life and took him in. "Everything is ready to test."

"What we have is: the wind spins the blades which creates the power, and that power is stored in the twelve volt batteries. We can't use twelve volts though, so it then goes into the inverter, which turns it into 120 volts, and that we can use. I hope everyone remembered to shut off everything in their domes. We don't want a power surge." Aaron faced the wall of breakers and started flipping switches. The first one lit up the generator room.

"Aaron," Gwen said. "What if there isn't any wind?"

"The batteries store the power for when there isn't any input. That shouldn't be a problem though, not here. It's always windy at the level the propellers are. Plus even a small breeze spins them. My biggest concern was *too* much wind. However, these newer units have built-in governors, and they can't go over a certain speed."

"I would suggest we check out each dome," Jeff said jubilantly.

"Just so you know, Jeff, I've only turned on the well pump and the two condo domes for now. The office and restaurant area can be tested later."

In each dome, they plugged in lamps and switched on overhead lights. They plugged the refrigerators and stoves back in.

"Why aren't those working Aaron?" Jeff asked.

"All the stoves have electronic ignitions, and the electronics have fried. I might be able to bypass the ignitions, I'm not sure though. The refrigerators are the same, too many circuits."

"What about the water heaters?" Adele asked hopefully.

"First we need water," Jeff said, standing by the sink. He turned the faucet on. It sputtered and spit. He turned it off.

"Leave it on, Jeff, there's air in the lines," Aaron said. Within a minute, the ice cold water was flowing. The group of seven people were mesmerized by the water coming out of the faucet.

"Correct me if I'm wrong, Aaron, but we'll have to be cautious about using too many things at one time, right," Jeff said, and Aaron nodded. "Since we are all heating with wood right now, I say we leave the furnaces off. Can we use the water heaters by lowering the heat and maybe shutting them off?"

"That would be a good solution. I was going to suggest rotating every six hours on the water heaters, alternating between the two units. That way the water doesn't cool off too much and everyone has warm to hot water. I know I'm sure looking forward to a hot shower!" Aaron opened what looked like a closet door, exposing the water heating unit. He dialed it down and plugged it in. Nothing happened. He unplugged it again. "We'll check out the schematics. There may be an electronic ignition in this too, I don't remember."

"Well, we have lights and we have water. Two things we didn't have yesterday. I say it's still cause for a celebration," Chet said. "Plug the clocks back in. Dinner is at six o'clock."

"I'm disappointed we don't have the hot water back so you can take a shower," Jeff said after the others had left.

"Me too, although I have another idea," Adele said, sitting down at her drawing table. She pulled out a fresh sheet of paper and began to draw. Jeff leaned over her shoulder.

"Ingenious," he said. "I've no doubt Aaron could make that in fifteen minutes or less. Let's take this drawing over to him right now. Maybe we will all get showers before dinner anyway."

"We better put more water on to heat, then!"

"This is so simple I don't know why we didn't come up with it before," Aaron said looking at Adele's design. "All we need is a plastic bucket, a hose, a clamp and a shower head."

"And a strong hook for the ceiling," Jeff added.

The two men, along with Walter, rummaged around in Aaron's massive workshop and found everything they needed to construct two shower buckets. With a short length of tubing glued into the hole drilled at the bottom on the side of the bucket and a small shower head attached to the other end, they were done.

In Jeff and Adele's condo, Aaron found a stud in the ceiling of the shower stall and secured the heavy duty hook that would hold the weight of the full bucket. Adele added the hot water and adjusted the temperature by adding some cold. Jeff lifted the bucket onto the hook and released the vise-like clamp on the hose, and water sprinkled out of the showerhead. He put the clamp back on to stop the gravity flow.

"Okay, men," Adele said, giggling, "Out! I'm taking a shower!"

She came out of the bathroom toweling her hair and smiled at Jeff. "That was the best shower ever." She kissed him soundly. "Your turn."

Chet insisted on pouring the champagne himself. He raised his glass and said, "To Aaron and Walter, who have given us back lights!" Everyone raised their glass and toasted the two men. "And to Adele, who has given us back the civilized function of taking a shower!"

CHAPTER TWENTY-SEVEN

"Zeke? Where are you?" Sheriff Burns called into the dark Walstroms store. He flashed the weakening beam of light across the entrance, thinking he should replace the batteries soon. The light was strong enough though to catch on the shoe of the man lying on the floor. He knelt down beside the body and felt for a pulse. When he couldn't feel one, he gently turned Zeke onto his back, exposing the long, jagged gash up his belly.

Claude stood and backed away, scanning the darkness beyond for any possible light. Not seeing any, he still pulled his service revolver before stepping into the gloom.

"Zeke is dead?" Henry gasped.

Claude ran his hand over his face. "Yeah, knifed in the belly. I also found the body of a kid by the pharmacy, also knifed. The kid was wearing a ski mask and may have been one of the attackers, who was then eliminated." He stared up at the ceiling. "What's happening to our town, Henry? These are peaceful, hardworking people. I've never known any of them to be violent, with the exception of the occasional bar-brawl, and certainly not killers."

"People do strange things during a time of crisis, you know that, Claude. If that youngster was in on a robbery of some sort, likely the others are young, too." The mayor looked past his friend to see Allison putting another log in the woodstove. "What is the status of the pharmacy?"

"Everything was moved to the hospital two days ago. It's in a locked room with the hospital's regular drug supply. Do you think we're going to need to post guards?"

"Perhaps. If these kids were after drugs, they might get desperate enough to try anything."

"Well, we certainly don't want to lose one of our doctors or nurses to some druggie. I'll set up a schedule and make sure everyone is armed. I hate this kind of shit." The sheriff stood and went back to his own office.

Later that night, Sarah Hughes heard a knock on her front door. "Oh, how nice to see you, come in, dear, it's cold out. Would you like some tea?"

Sarah Hughes' body was found the next day when Mike Miller delivered wood to her house. Her throat had been neatly sliced open. There were no signs of a struggle.

"Sarah is dead now too?" Henry sighed, leaning back in his overstuffed leather office chair.

"Whoever did this wasn't a stranger. She knew the person and let them in. There were two teacups at the table and the pocketknife used was left in the sink. It had Sarah's initials engraved on the handle. Unfortunately there is no way for us to lift fingerprints, and somehow I don't think there are any besides Sarah's," Claude said.

"I think we need to spread the news that everyone living alone needs to either pair up, or be ultra-cautious letting people in," Henry suggested. "What's the situation with the hospital?"

"I had a deputy there all night. With a lantern burning, he was real obvious to anyone that might have come around, so it was quiet. I don't know how long that can last, though. My men are complaining about the extra duty and being away from their own families," Claude said. "And I think the sooner we finish getting the food out of Walstroms, the better. Without food or drugs in there, it will be less appealing."

"Someone at the meeting suggested to me later that we could reopen that small grocery at Cliff and Main, and stock the food there. It's more visible and less vulnerable than Walstroms."

"I like that idea, Henry. I've been thinking too, that the people need to do more to help. What do you think about having all who are interested to meet us at Walstroms and they can fill a grocery cart with what they need? Then they can wheel the cart home to unload," Claude suggested. "When everyone has a supply, we take the rest to that grocery. There's a lot of food available and we can't afford to lose any of it."

"I like that. We'll put the word out. I've set up a message board at the churches, the café, and of course here. Let's do it soon, maybe tomorrow. That will give everyone time to shovel the snow off their walks. It won't be easy pushing those carts if they don't," Henry said.

"Have you two noticed the sky today?" Allison asked from the doorway. "It looks like a storm is on the way, maybe another day or two."

"We better get some notices up in the next hour, and schedule the cart-brigade for tomorrow early," Henry said with a heavy sigh. "Without plows, any storm is going to be a bad one. People need to be ready."

"Allison, honey, I can shovel the walk," Claude said when he was leaving home after lunch.

"You go do the offices, I'll do this. Now shoo!" She picked up another shovel full and tossed it to the side. He chuckled at her determination and hurried away. He stopped to talk with Mae, who continued toward her.

"Hi, Mae," Allison greeted the waitress from the café.

"Hi. Was the sheriff just here?" she asked hesitantly.

"Yes, dear, Claude has moved in with me, finally," Allison laughed. "And the mayor is staying in our guest room. It isn't good for anyone to be alone now."

"I'm glad you have someone here. Now I don't have to worry about you." Mae looked up the street seeing others shovel their walks.

"What about you?"

"Oh, I'm okay. Dad is hanging on. I better go and help with the shoveling. There are a couple of people who need a younger back to help out. See ya."

Allison watched the young woman leave, thinking it a strange visit.

"This is a good turnout, Henry. How did we reach so many people so quickly?" Claude asked the mayor.

"I gave a stack of notices to Allison to put up, and a bunch to Mae to pass out. Looks to be a hundred people, maybe more, and I see some brought wagons. It's good to see people taking initiative," Henry answered. He climbed up onto a chair to address the crowd. "I hope we have enough carts for everyone. If not, take what you can carry and come back for a second load. I want everyone to be polite about this and don't take more than your share. There are deputies and volunteer guards in all the aisles to help you. Please shop quickly since there are more people coming." He stepped down and people rushed into the store.

The process went smoothly, with only one or two arguments over an item. After an hour, the last person was leaving.

"That's an interesting assortment, Mae," Claude commented.

"Oh, this is for George Green," she replied, looking at the basket full of soups, macaroni and cheese mixes, and tuna fish. "When I was helping him shovel yesterday he said he didn't think he could walk this far, so I said I would get his share and he wanted things easy to heat or fix. That's okay isn't it? I'll need to come back for things for me and Dad."

"That was nice of you to help him out, Mae. The more people help each other the better off we all will be."

"I'm still worried about him, Sheriff. Since he lives alone, I suggested he either stay with someone, or have a friend move in with him. He's a stubborn one though, says he likes living alone. Maybe he would listen to you," she said.

"That's a good idea, I'll talk to him."

"If you don't mind, with this storm coming and all, I'd really like to get my stuff early and get on home. Would you take this basket to George and talk with him?"

"Absolutely, Mae." Claude turned to Henry. "I'm taking this over to George, and Mae is going back in for more for herself. I'll be back in a half hour or so. Allison, wait up! I'll walk with you."

Claude and Allison wrestled their carts through the snow, and after Allison turned off Main Street toward her home, Claude continued another block.

"George? It's Sheriff Burns. I've brought a cart of food for you," he called out and knocked on the door. "George?" The house was unusually quiet. Claude tried the door, and, finding it unlocked like so many in town, he let himself in. In the small dining room, the sheriff found George's body, still sitting in the straight back chair. His throat had been slit by something very sharp. In the kitchen sink was a bloody box cutter.

The bile rose in Claude's throat at the smell of death: the coppery scent of blood and the stench of the body systems letting go. Lividity had already set in; death had occurred sometime during the night. He stepped back out into the fresh, cold air and closed the door behind him, pushing the cart back down street with a heavy heart.

"Sheriff!" Mae called out, wheeling her own cart and noticing the still full basket pushed by the sheriff. "Wasn't George home?"

"When was the last time you talked with George?" he asked.

"Yesterday afternoon when I shoveled his walk. Why?"

"Don't go in there; it's now a crime scene. George was murdered during the night."

Mae gasped and covered her mouth in horror.

"I'm going to take his cart over to the café. All this soup should come in handy for feeding a few people," Claude told her.

Mae only nodded, and continued on to the home she shared with her elderly father.

Henry was shocked at the news of the friendly older man being murdered.

"It's got to be the same person, Henry: same method, same disposal of the weapon, same lack of any struggle. We have a serial killer on our hands, and it's one of us."

The second half of the food dispersal was somber as the news of yet another murder spread through the town.

"Another cart full, Allison?" Henry questioned, seeing her back in the store.

"Henry Hawkins, you do recall that there are three of us in the house now and each of us are entitled to some of this food like everyone else, right?" she snapped at him.

"Yes, ma'am, I know that."

She took a deep breath. "I'm sorry for snapping like that, it's just…" she swiped at an errant tear. "I liked old George. He was my middle school math teacher and a really nice person." She pushed the cart at Henry. "Here, you fill this one up and try for some meat if there's any left. I'm going to fill this one for the church." Allison wandered off in search of blankets and towels and to be alone.

Claude found Allison in the housewares department, sitting on the floor next to an empty shopping cart. He sat on the floor beside her and pulled her into his arms. The dam burst and she sobbed into his chest. When the tears subsided, he stood and helped her up. He reached into a display and tore open a package of cloth napkins, handing her one.

"Sheriff Burns, isn't that theft?" she tried, failing at the joke.

He smiled down at her. "Rank has its privileges, Allison."

"It will be strange when we are all equals," she said. Squaring her shoulders, she began piling the cart with blankets, towels and pillows, all destined for the warming center at the church.

"We need one more cart of food for the church, Claude. I know there isn't much left and that's good, but they're going to be feeding a lot of folks, especially during this storm."

He looked out the large plate glass windows that covered the front of Walstroms. The sunlight that filtered in was starting to dim. "It looks like it will start soon. I think it's time to wrap things up in here. You go on now, take that to the church and then go home and lock the doors. Don't let anyone in, and I mean *no one*, I don't care

176

who it is, until me or Henry get there. Understand?" He looked hard at her. "*Understand?*" She nodded silently. "I know the church needs extra food, but so does the hospital. I'll drop this cart off there and be home shortly."

"Here's extra food, Doc. I tried for soft and easy: soups, pasta, hot cereal like oatmeal," Claude said, pushing the full cart into the emergency room.

"Thanks, Claude, I appreciate it," Dr. Sam said. "Have a seat for a minute. I have an update on the man you brought in." They sat on the hard plastic chairs that lined the large waiting room and faced each other. "While there was enough sunlight coming in, I did surgery on Mr. Polez. I'll be honest, it made me really nervous doing such delicate work in a non-sterile environment. I had Ellen assist me and my only other nurse stood guard, making sure no one came in with further contamination.

"Anyway, I removed one toe from his left foot and two from the right. He'll limp, but he'll walk."

"What about his hands?"

"I think he must have had his left hand under his body, and that little body heat helped. I removed only the tip of the pinky. The rest will be fine. His right hand is another story. The tips of all four fingers were lost down to the first knuckle, and the tip of the thumb is gone. I'll keep an eye on that hand for another week to see if that was the extent of the damage."

"Speaking of another week, are you going to be okay in here for that long?" Claude asked.

"No, we're not. That heater is great, though it is barely keeping it fifty degrees in here. We're going to have to figure something else, Claude, and soon. I'm open to any ideas you have."

"I'm going to scout the houses close to Main Street, see what's empty that has wood heat. I can't get you moved for a few days though, not with this storm coming in," the sheriff said.

"I can hold out for a few more days. Oh, and we lost Mabel this morning, so there are only four patients to move, plus some equipment."

During the short walk home, Claude noticed the increase of wind and then the snow began to fall. The afternoon storm hit with a fury common to the Rocky Mountains.

CHAPTER TWENTY-EIGHT

Dr. Sam Cory made his rounds in the early daylight. The storm was still howling after three days, and the daylight was merely a brighter hue to the blankness of the snow.

Kyle moaned softly when he tried moving.

"Mr. Polez, are you awake?" the doctor asked cautiously. "Kyle?" he asked again, hoping the more familiar name might rouse the patient.

Kyle blinked his eyes and looked around. "Where am I?" he croaked out and winced with pain.

"Don't try to talk yet," Dr. Cory warned. "Your throat is likely dry and sore. I'll bring you some water." Soon after, the nurse, Nancy Tibbs, was at his side with a bottle of water and a flexible straw.

"Take only small sips to start, Mr. Polez, not too much." She held the straw to his lips, his pale blue eyes fixed on her face and her short blonde hair. "Yes, that's good, just a little more." She set the bottle on the table next to him and backed away, his eyes followed her.

"Does your throat feel better now?" Dr. Cory asked.

Kyle nodded. "Where?"

"You're in a hospital in the town of Avon, Montana. You were found buried in the snow at the outer edge of an avalanche. Do you remember any of that?"

Kyle shook his head and closed his eyes briefly. They called him Kyle and that sounded familiar but he couldn't remember anything else. "How long?" he whispered.

"You've been here for over a week now. It was pretty touch and go there for a while. You were half frozen when the sheriff brought you in. You were lucky they found you when they did. Another twelve hours and you would've been dead." The doctor stood. "You rest now. I'll be back later." He picked up the chart hanging from the metal post at the end of the bed and walked to abandoned desk where he could sit and make notes on Kyle's progress.

Kyle looked around the room, noting the high ceiling and stainless, unlit light fixtures. There were two other beds that he could see, although there could be more, he couldn't move his head far. The air smelled cool and oily to him. He closed his eyes and was quickly asleep.

"Do you think he'll be alright, Sam?" Ellen asked, placing her hands on his shoulders, massaging them gently.

"It's too early to tell. Physically he might recover, although the real test will be mentally, when discovers the amputations." Sam swiveled the chair to face her. She leaned down and gently kissed him.

"I wish we didn't have to keep our marriage a secret, Sam," Ellen frowned.

They'd had a small wedding over the summer, and decided it best to stay quiet about it lest the hospital administrators transferred one of them.

"As soon as Claude gets us moved into a house and we get the patients settled, we'll tell everyone. How's that?"

"I'd like that." She backed away when she heard Nancy pushing the morning cart down the hall.

Allison stood gazing out at the falling snow. "Claude, does it look like it's letting up some to you?" she asked hopefully.

He came up behind her, sliding his arms around her waist, and rested his chin on the top of her blonde head. "Actually, it does. This has been a long snowstorm, and I'm ready for it to end."

"Me too," Henry said from the table where they had all just finished their lunch of soup and toast. "I like you two, but I'm getting tired of gin rummy."

Two hours later the snow had completely stopped, although the wind continued to push the drifts around until midnight. The stars sparkled in the night sky brighter than anyone remembered.

Henry and Claude tramped through the knee deep snow to the town offices. By nine in the morning the sun was blinding in its brilliance, making both wish they had not forgotten their sunglasses.

"Three days without heat in here could mean trouble for the plumbing," Henry said.

"Nope, I already drained the pipes. I'll get a fire going and then we need to check out a couple of houses on Main or near Main for the hospital to move into. They aren't going to last much longer where they are."

"Did you also ask Mike to bring his horses back in after the storm was over?"

"Got it done, Henry, stop worrying. I do need to find someone to relieve the deputy I had stay to guard the pharmacy, though. Once we move them, they should be safer."

"Doc, we've found a four bedroom bungalow with a loft and a basement. It was one of the homes occupied by snowbirds, and I doubt they'll be coming back any time soon," Henry explained to Sam Cory.

"Excellent! When can I see it?"

"We can go right now, it's only a few blocks away, just off Main on Carlisle," Claude replied. "And the best part is it's mostly furnished."

"Doctor, Mr. Polez is awake again and complaining about the pain in his hands," Nancy said.

"Can we talk to him?" Claude asked.

"Let me check him over first, and give him a shot of morphine, then you can question him. You can come with me now if you like, just hang back, okay?" Dr. Cory led them to the far side of the room and stepped around a modesty screen. "Mr. Polez, I'm glad to see you awake again. The nurse said you're experiencing some pain. Where?"

"My right hand. I can't move my fingers and they really hurt," Kyle complained.

"I see. I'll give you something for the pain and then we need to talk," the doctor said. "This is Sheriff Claude Burns, who found you, and this is Mayor Henry Hawkins. They'd like to ask you a few questions." Sam Cory backed away to give Ellen room to administer the shot. Kyle stared at her quietly. Something about her blonde hair was familiar to him.

"Mr. Polez, do you remember anything about the avalanche? We found you buried about a half mile south of the Geo Dome Resort," Claude asked.

"I can't help you, Sheriff. They say my name is Kyle Polez, and it sounds familiar, but I don't remember anything else."

"Kyle, remember that I said you were half frozen when they brought you in? I meant that literally. I'm going to remove the bandages from your right hand. There was extensive damage from frostbite," Dr. Sam talked as he cut away the wrapping, exposing the inch and a half nubs that used to be his fingers.

Kyle gasped at all the stitches covering what remained of his hand, and then he passed out from shock.

"Ellen, I want you to keep him sedated. I'm going to look at this house they have for us."

Dr. Sam left with Claude and Henry.

"The place is perfect, Ellen. There are three bedrooms on the main floor; two have two twin beds and the other has bunk beds. I think we can take those down and make that a surgery. There's the upstairs loft that we can use, and the finished basement would be a good place for the pharmacy and any other staff, like Nancy," Dr. Sam said to his wife. "Since the wood burner is in the living room, I think for now we should line up the beds there to take advantage of the heat. Those bedrooms might be too cold right now, although they'll be fine after the weather breaks."

"The couple that lived there had a lot of family that would vacation with them and set it up for drop in guests. The living room might eventually make a good waiting room or reception area," Claude said.

"Where are the owners now?" Ellen asked.

"They're snowbirds, and I think they winter in Arizona. They stopped at my office to tell me they were leaving, so I know they left in October," Claude answered. "I don't keep track of where everyone goes, though. We have around five hundred that leave for the winter. I usually get cellphone numbers in case of an emergency, but cells don't tell me where they are."

Four of the community women cleaned the house quickly, moved and made all the beds, readying them for the patients. The move took the rest of the day once Mike came into town with the wagon and his team of horses.

"Since you'll be staying at the house too, Nancy, we wanted you to be the first to know something," Dr. Sam said.

"Sam and I got married last July," Ellen said. "We've been keeping it quiet, but there isn't any need to anymore."

"I'm so happy for you," Nancy said, giving them both a joyous hug. "I've noticed how chummy you two seem, so it makes sense to me now. And thank you for telling me first."

Jerry Collins sat in his wheelchair at the kitchen table playing solitaire and waiting for his daughter Mae to come home. He heard the back door open.

"It's about time you got home. I messed in my pants again; you need to clean me up right now!" he demanded. She came up behind him and smoothed his wiry gray hair down. Suddenly she grabbed a fist full of the thin hair and jerked his head back. In one quick move she drew the straight-razor across his throat, ending his constant complaining.

Mae dropped the razor in the kitchen sink and left.

Dr. Cory let himself into the café where his friend Mae worked. Her eyes lit up when she saw him and quickly checked her reflection to make sure her makeup was still perfect. She knew he was older than her, and that it wasn't right to fall in love with your doctor, but she had.

"Hi, Dr. Cory. I haven't seen much of you since this power thing. It's good to see you." Mae tried to be as cordial as possible while her heart beat erratically just being near him. "Can I get you some coffee?"

"No thanks, Mae. I came for a favor."

"Anything for you, Sam," she slipped, calling him by his first name, something she did only in her fantasies.

"We're going to have a small reception at our new location, and I'd like it if you could come up with some simple catering for the event. It's a double celebration, really." His eyes twinkled with inner happiness. "The moving of the hospital of course, and the announcement that Ellen and I got married."

"M-m-married?" Mae stammered. Her fantasy world began to crumble.

"We were married last July, but we've kept it a secret. Now that we don't have to, we're going to announce it to everyone. You're one of the first to know."

"Married," she repeated quietly, struggling to keep a neutral expression. "Congratulations, Dr. Cory. I'll see what I can come up with." Her grip on reality started to slip even more. "Oh, and can I ask you to stop and see my dad? He's been complaining about his chest hurting again. I don't like leaving him alone all the time. Since I have to be here, though, I don't have much choice. Opening up at seven in the morning and then not having anyone to relieve me makes for a really long day."

"Of course I will. Your place is only a few houses down now. I'll stop on my way back," Sam said. "And, Mae, thanks. You're a good friend."

CHAPTER TWENTY-NINE

Jeff and Adele made their way to the other dome across the freshly fallen snow. The recent blizzard had dumped twenty inches on them and their snowshoes sunk eight inches with each step.

"Come on in, boss-man," Aaron said, opening the door. "That was some storm. We'll have a lot of digging out to do to get back into the workshop."

"Which brings up a question, Aaron. Have you gotten any closer to the water heater issue?" Jeff asked, accepting a cup of coffee from Gwen.

"Yes and no," he answered. "I've carefully disassembled our water tank brain box over the past few days for something to do. However, when the circuits were fried so was the heating element. Sorry to say, I can't get them working again. I'm going to try the stove next, but I'm thinking that has even more complicated wiring, so I don't have high hopes."

"That's disappointing." Jeff sighed. "At least you tried."

"Now that the snow has stopped and we can get out again, I'd like to cook us a nice dinner," Chet said, hoping to cheer up everyone. "Do you remember what tomorrow is?"

"Tomorrow?" Adele furrowed her forehead in thought.

Chet grinned. "It's New Year's Eve!"

"How is it we still have so much wine, Jeff?" Adele asked as they were selecting the various wines to go with dinner.

"I had already restocked the cellar before Thanksgiving, getting ready for the winter season. Winter here is just as busy as summer, only I usually have more couples and fewer families, and I'm always at capacity. That's twelve hotel rooms and six domes, which is a minimum of eighteen couples per *day*. There are only seven of us now. The wine will last a long time," Jeff explained. "Chet suggested two bottles of white, three of red, and three champagnes. That's more than a bottle person. I think it's going to be a tipsy party." He laughed.

"Do you know what he's preparing?"

"Nope, I do know it's going to be great though. Chet really is an amazing chef. I'm lucky to have hired him away from a place in New York. Of course, I doubled his salary to do it."

"Did you double Aaron's salary, too?"

"I didn't have to. Aaron and I went to school together. We've been best friends for a long time, ever since we were kids. I think he would work for free just to work here doing whatever he wants to. That I won millions of dollars is secondary, the bond is our friendship," Jeff said, wheeling the heavy cart to the recently dug out entrance.

Back at the condo where dinner would be, they pushed the champagne and the white wine into a mound of snow to chill and took the red inside.

At seven o'clock, Jeff and Adele snowshoed the short distance to join their friends. Adele had insisted on wearing a skirt and was forced to walk a bit slower than normal to hold the hem up so she wouldn't trip.

Jeff uncorked the well chilled chardonnay to serve with the crab-stuffed pasta appetizer, and the pureed pumpkin soup.

"Save room for the main course," Chet warned. In the center of the large wooden table he placed a whole tenderloin, seasoned and grilled to perfection, garnished with jarred spiced crabapple slices and a side dish of cheesy potato puffs. Jeff poured the red wine for everyone.

With dinner over and full champagne flutes now in front of everyone, Walter stood to propose a toast.

"I want to take this opportunity to thank each one of you for taking me in like you did. You would have been in your rights to shoot me. Now, I don't want to sound ungrateful, but I'm going to leave."

The protests and questions came from everyone.

"Please, let me finish," Walter said. "Gwen and I have decided to walk into Avon tomorrow. It's only ten miles, so we should make it easily in one day."

"Why?" Adele asked, looking at Gwen.

"It's so hard not knowing what's going on," she pleaded. "What if things are back to normal elsewhere?"

"What if they're worse, Gwen?" Beth said.

"Then they're worse, and we might be back." Gwen brushed a tear from her cheek. "You have all been so wonderful to me, but I miss my family. I want to try and reach them."

The sun rose in the morning to a brilliant blue sky. In spite of the gorgeous weather, the day was somber.

"I've packed several sandwiches for you," Chet said, obviously distressed, "and bottles of water." He set the two full backpacks on the table and stepped back.

"You'll need these," Jeff said, handing them two pairs of sunglasses.

Aaron stood in front of them, checking out their gear. "Boots are good, jackets look appropriate, two pair of gloves, and hats with ear flaps. Good." He put his hands on his hips and glared at the two. "I don't like this one bit, not one bit. Please, be careful." His lower lip quivered ever so slightly.

Adele and Beth took their turns giving hugs and then helped with the backpacks.

"When you get into town, go to the town offices and find Sheriff Burns. He'll help you," Jeff said. "And you *can* come back, anytime you want to."

The five remaining survivors kept their eyes on the pair until they were out of sight.

Ten hours later, Gwen and Walter were snowshoeing down the middle of Main Street and went into the Sheriff's office.

"Sheriff Burns? My name is Gwen Swanson. We walked down from the Geo Dome Resort."

"Come in! I've tried getting up there to see how Jeff is doing but got stopped by that avalanche. How is it up there?" Claude asked.

"There have been some problems. We got through them okay, though. I'm Walter Singleton." He held out his hand. "Can you tell us anything about what's going on outside? We've been six weeks without any information."

"It's late in the day. Why don't you two come home with me for supper and I'll tell you what I can. We'll find you a place to stay tomorrow," Claude offered.

"Sheriff!" Dr. Cory burst into the office. "We've got another one! Jerry Collins."

CHAPTER THIRTY

"Another one what?" Walter asked, pulling Gwen closer to him.

"I'll explain later," Claude said. "Doc, does Mae know?"

"I thought you might want to tell her."

"How did you find him?"

"I stopped at the café to talk to Mae about something and she asked me to check on him since she's stuck there all day and he was alone," Dr. Cory explained. "His throat was slit and a bloody straight razor is in the sink. I didn't touch anything, not that it would make any difference." When he saw Walter and Gwen flinch, he said, "Sorry, I should have waited with that piece of information."

"You go back to your patients, Doc, I'll go see Mae, *after* we remove the body." Claude lowered his head to his chest. "Henry, can you come out here please?" he called out.

"Hello, I'm Mayor Henry Hawkins," Henry smiled, holding out his hand to the new couple. "Did I hear Sam say something about another one? I hope that's not what I think it means."

"I'm afraid so. Jerry Collins. I need to get Deputy Teagan to help me, and then I'll talk to Mae," Claude said. "These two folks walked down from the Dome Resort, Henry. I promised them some of Allison's good cooking and a place to stay for the night. Could you take care of that for me?"

Claude noticed Mae's reaction when he told her the news, and he found it quite unexpected.

Mae scrunched up her face and looked down. When she lifted her head, she was composed. "I'm sure you're finding it odd that I'm not weeping, Sheriff. My father was old and sick, and I resigned myself to his death quite some time ago. That he would go in such a violent manner is terrible. However, he was also a cruel and mean man and I'm not sorry he's gone. My life will be much easier now. Does that make me a bad person, Sheriff?"

"No, Mae, it doesn't. I'm surprised, that's all. We've already removed the body and taken it to the new morgue outside of town. If you wish to see him, I will arrange that," he said.

"No, that's okay. I have my last memory of him sleeping peacefully and I will hold onto that."

Claude nodded. "If you need anything, come down to the township office and we will do what we can."

"Thank you."

When the sheriff closed the door behind him, Mae smiled.

CHAPTER THIRTY-ONE

The gas station on the south side of town where Adele had stopped for directions that first day was not open. Anything that needed gasoline to run didn't work, with or without fuel. The station was, however, occupied.

The station was home to Taylor Mayde, one of the few auto mechanics in town, and he was known as the best who could fix anything. Forty-year-old Taylor had converted an old fuel oil burner so it took used motor oil. He had an endless supply of the dirty fluid and consequently, an endless supply of comfortable heat. After the EMP hit, the young woman he had running the desk and register asked if she could stay since she had no place to go.

Jane Jones hated her name and had gone by JJ ever since she was a child. Taylor was a nice man to work for. He wasn't mean like her father and he never yelled at her. When Taylor agreed to let her stay, she willingly agreed to share his bed. It was a good arrangement for both of them. JJ was a better-than-average cook, and Taylor was a gentle lover.

Taylor was also the local pot dealer. He grew his marijuana plants behind the station in an area that was prolific with the tall weeds that disguised his product. With an easy and cheap source of pot, Taylor had a ready supply of cash during good times and a steady supply of food in the current bad times.

The building roar of engines caught the attention of Taylor long before JJ even heard them. "Looks like we might have some customers for gas, JJ. I wonder what they have for trade. You stay behind the counter; I'll watch from the bays."

Six brightly painted antique snowmobiles slowed and pulled into the closed gas station. The men dismounted like they were accustomed to getting off of motorcycles. From the saddlebag of the first in line, a large meaty guy produced a long hose and a primer bulb. Two others lifted shovels and started clearing patches looking for the main intake cap used by the tankers to fill the underground storage tanks. Once found, they filled the tanks of the sleds and began filling two five gallon containers.

"Hey! You gonna pay for that or what?" JJ shouted from the doorway. All six men turned in her direction. Too late, she realized she should have kept quiet.

"Jack, why don't you go... *pay* the lady," the leader said.

Jack, six foot tall and muscular, sauntered toward the door. Even though JJ tried to lock the heavy glass door, her hands were shaking and Jack pushed his way in. He was met with a shotgun in his face held by Taylor.

"Hey, man, I was just coming in to ask how much we owed for the gas. We didn't know anyone was here," Jack hurriedly explained, his beady eyes scanning the room.

"What have you got to barter? Not many are taking cash anymore," Taylor said.

"Let me go ask the guys." He backed out of the store and returned to his sled. Taylor could see him talking with the others, but couldn't hear what was being said.

"I was met with a shotgun. Guy holding it wants to barter."

"I say we take off; what's he going to do?" Enno said. As the unofficial leader of their small gang, he usually made the decisions, however he was smart enough to know that when one of the others had a better idea, it was good to acknowledge that, and go with the flow. He found it helped keep their fluctuating loyalty.

"Here's something else to consider, Enno: the guy with the shotgun reeked of pot. He's got a stash in there, I just know it."

"Hmm, that's an interesting twist," Enno said. "Okay, guys, here's what we're gonna do." They whispered their plans, and the others agreed. Enno got a package from his saddlebag and headed toward the office with Jack by his side.

"Hi, there," Enno said. "I understand you want to barter for the gas. That sounds good to me." He walked up to the counter and set the box down. "We've been collecting a few items along our way for moments like this." He unlatched the box and laid pieces of jewelry on the counter. Diamond bracelets, ruby and emerald earrings, all sparkling brilliantly in the hazy sunlight. "What would the pretty lady like?"

JJ's eyes were big and round as she stared at the gems. She glanced over at Taylor. He smiled and nodded. She picked up a gold choker necklace inlaid with diamonds and sapphires. "The lady has good taste," Enno said with a wicked grin. "Does that satisfy for the gas?" he asked Taylor.

"If JJ is happy with it, yes."

"Now, I can tell by the heavenly scent in the air that you might have something else we'd be interested in," Enno continued. "What about the matching earrings for an ounce?"

"Half ounce," Taylor said.

"Deal. Can we try some, to make sure we're getting a decent product?" Jack asked amiably.

The others, Bill, Bob, Ross, and Derick, were summoned in and they all retreated to the warmth of the empty bays. Passing a joint around mellowed everyone and Taylor gradually let his guard down.

"JJ, go get one of those twelve packs to share with our new friends, would you?"

"Beer?" Enno said. "JJ just might get the matching bracelet." He laughed, knowing what they ultimately had in mind.

"How did you guys come across six working old snowmobiles?" Taylor asked, popping open a cold beer.

"Right place at the right time, I guess you could say," Jack answered. "We were at an antique snowmobile show checking out the newer sleds when the EMP hit. They were the only things left that even started. It took some tinkering to get them to run smooth, but Bill's good at things like that."

"Where'd you get all the jewelry?" JJ asked, fingering the necklace that was secured around her neck.

"You'd be surprised what people will trade when their lives depend on it." Enno said, leaving the implication hang in the air.

Taylor rolled another joint and passed it around. By the time it made it back to him, he was asleep in his chair.

"This looks like a nice situation, guys, maybe we should stay for a day or two. We've got beer, pot, food," Enno said, looking at JJ, "and some young pussy. Tie and gag this loser." He walked over to the glassy eyed girl and slapped her hard. She collapsed without a sound. He yanked her warm sweatpants off and raped her.

One at a time, each one took a turn with the young woman.

"That was fun," Jack said when the others were done. "I think I'll have another round with that piece of tail. Now where did she go?" He found her hiding behind a desk, clutching her torn pants and sobbing. "Come on out, little girl, you don't want to make me mad." He grabbed her foot with his big hand and dragged her out. She kicked at him and he laughed. "Ah, you want to play rough now, eh? I like it when they fight." He lowered his zipper slowly and pulled himself out. JJ's eyes went wide with shock at how big he was. This time he raped her slow and hard. When he was done, he pulled the earrings off, tearing her lobes, but took care to unlatch the necklace. He handed them back to Enno, who put them back in the box of stolen goods.

The six men stayed the night, eating, drinking, and smoking their way through Taylor's stash, taking a break only to satisfy their lust, while Taylor was forced to watch. At noon on the second day, they packed up the bundles of marijuana, a couple of bottles of whiskey, and what was left of the food.

Enno squatted down in front of Taylor. "Thanks for the hospitality." He pulled a long, sharp knife from his boot and placed it midway on Taylor's belly. Very slowly he pushed it in, seeing his victim's eyes silently scream with pain. He stood, and drew the blade upward.

When Enno handed Jack the knife, he knew they couldn't leave any witnesses. He took the knife and led JJ into the other room where he cut off one of her hands.

She crawled back into the warmth of the bays. Wrapped in a blanket, she bled to death a few hours later.

"I hear engines," Claude said from behind his desk. He stood and saw the six snowmobiles drive by and stop at the café. He shrugged on his leather jacket and grabbed his shotgun. Opening the door, he saw the six big men dismount, holding rifles. Claude slipped back inside unnoticed, put on his previously unused tactical vest, and filled his pockets with ammo. One pocket with shells, the other with magazines for his service pistol. "Henry, keep Allison inside!"

He waited in his doorway until the men were inside the café and then he hurried as quickly and as quietly down the snow filled street as possible. He turned into the alleyway that ran behind the stores and found the back door he was looking for, cautiously stepping inside. Hearing voices, and Mae's strained comments, Claude removed his jacket and put on the nearest apron, tucking his pistol inside the bulletproof vest. He glanced through the small, dirty circular window of the door from the kitchen to assess the situation. The six men inside were still standing, rifles resting across an arm, fortunately not pointing in any direction. One of them stood looking out at the street, guarding the door.

Claude grabbed a large tray to hide the sawed off shotgun he held out of sight, and pushed the swinging door open.

"Say, Mae, your shift is over and I'm ready to relieve… whoa, new faces in town. Howdy, guys," he said innocently. "Can you lower those guns? We're a peaceful bunch."

The men eyed him and laughed. Jack was the first to try raising his rifle. Claude pulled the trigger, blasting him back into the empty tables. Mae dropped to the floor. He swung the barrel toward the remaining two men. "Drop the rifles, nice and easy."

"Why did you shoot him? We didn't come here looking for trouble, man," Enno said, lowering the rifle that was still clutched tightly in his hands.

"I said to drop it," Claude's voice was low and menacing.

"Where's the law when you need it?" the big guy said with a smirk and began raising his gun.

Mae stood. "Right where *I* need him. Thanks, Sheriff."

"Sheriff?"

"I hate repeating myself, asshole. Drop the guns, *now*."

The smirk was replaced with a blank glare and guns landed on the floor.

"Now turn around and go out the door, one at a time, slowly," Claude said, coming around the edge of the counter.

Enno was the last to leave, and at the last minute he pivoted, pulling a handgun from his waistband, and fired at the sheriff from less than ten feet. Claude staggered backward against the counter and fell. Enno grabbed their rifles and fled.

The sleds fired up instantly and the men took off, leaving Jack behind.

Mae came out from hiding and knelt beside Claude, weeping. Claude opened his eyes and said, "Help me up." Seated on one of the counter stools, he ripped off the dirty apron and undid the straps on his dented bulletproof vest. "Oh, that hurts," he said, rubbing his chest. "Mae, would you get Dr. Cory? I want this piece of shit alive." He glared at the inert Jack.

"Good thing you had birdshot in that shotgun," Sam said to Claude, checking the wounds on Jack's torso. A deputy stood silently beside the prisoner, the zip-tie handcuffs already in place. "I'm surprised though that you used something that wasn't lethal."

"Just the first shot, Sam, as a warning. The rest would take down a moose." Claude stood and winced.

"Sit down, Sheriff, and let me look." The doctor examined him front and back. "You're going to have one hell of a bruise, my friend, but it's better than being dead."

"I think the town council will let us each have one of these vests now," Claude chuckled.

The five snowmobiles sped out of town, veering off onto a road that looked recently used. Hog Back Road.

Enno slowed as houses began to appear off in the woods. He scanned each one quickly, looking for signs of occupants. The third one had smoke curling out from the tall red brick chimney, and Enno led his group up the short driveway. They jumped off the sleds as one and rushed the ornate door.

Cal, Fred, and four other young men were ready and met the intruders with guns aimed.

Enno stopped and held his hands out to his sides. "Well, well, looks like we've come across some like-minded souls." He assessed the group and took a cautious step forward. "What do you say we join forces? There's a lot to be had out there for a larger team."

Cal, knowing this was true, as they had recently joined up with the other three, said, "That's a possibility. What's in it for us? You got any drugs?"

Enno's group had been together for over a month and the pecking order was well established. With Jack gone, Derick was Enno's new right hand. He smiled, and pulled a baggie from his jacket pocket and tossed it to Cal. Cal stayed steady with his handgun and big Fred bent over and retrieved the package. He opened it and took a deep sniff. "This smells like some good shit, Cal."

The menacing force was now eleven strong.

Even though Enno was ten years older than Cal, he liked the young punk and took him aside to talk as the two leaders of their new group.

"You're from here, right? You must know the area real well. So what's up this road? Anything good?" Enno asked, passing Cal a bottle of spiced rum after taking a swig. "And what did you do with the owners of this house?"

"I didn't do anything with them. This is my house," the young man boasted. "We haven't been able to get far. The road is blocked by a wall of snow. Must have been an avalanche a few weeks ago, plus the recent blizzard keeps everyone from going anywhere. There's a resort up there somewhere," Cal told him.

"A resort? What kind of resort? One of those spa places where you sit in hot mud and get a massage?" Enno laughed.

"Naw, it's more like an outdoor retreat thing. Where people go hiking and shit like that. It's been open for a couple of years. Before my folks died they would go up there for dinner occasionally, real ritzy they said. And they said it looked weird too, because all the places were domes, built like igloos."

"When did your folks die, kid?"

"Mom died last year from cancer, and dad started drinking real heavy after that. He was in the hospital on life support for kidney failure when that EMP hit. He didn't make it. Doc said he was one of the first to go, and that he went peaceful. I guess that was good." Cal went quiet for a while, lost in his own thoughts.

"So there's a hospital in this Podunk town? Where there's a hospital there's drugs, you know." Enno was calculating how best to use this kid.

"Yeah, they recently closed it down and moved the few patients into a big house. The Walstroms had a pharmacy, but the sheriff got to it before we did, and moved it all someplace. At least, that's the word circulating."

"You're well spoken, Cal. I like that. You're smart and I like that too. Have you ever been in trouble before?" Enno was thinking that a local boy might be a good resource. For now.

"Have I *caused* trouble? Yeah, lots of it. Have I been caught? Never."

Enno laughed and slapped the boy on the back. "Now I really like you! I think we've got a good working relationship ahead of us. Let's go join the others."

Cal walked calmly into the big house that was now the new hospital, and rang the bell on the desk.

Dr. Cory came from behind the privacy screen that hid Kyle from view. "Cal, what can I do for you?"

"Hi, Dr. Cory. Ever since my dad died, I've been having some really fierce headaches. I had started walking down to Walstroms, when I remembered it's closed. I was wondering if you had any aspirin or something that would take the edge off so I could get some sleep," Cal lied smoothly.

"Of course, Cal, have a seat." Dr. Sam opened a door and descended into the basement where the new pharmacy was located. Moments later, he brought up a bottle of aspirin and an empty prescription bottle. He poured a dozen pills into the small orange bottle and handed it to the young orphan.

"Thanks, I'm sure this will help."

Cal's mission was complete. He discovered where the new pharmacy was located, and as a bonus, he had interesting information. There was a patient handcuffed to a bed.

Ellen Tibbs-Cory rushed into the sheriff's office only to find it locked and empty. She quickly backtracked and went to Allison's house and pounded on the door.

"Oh, Claude, thank goodness I found you! There was a break in last night." She stopped, trying to catch her breath.

"Where, Ellen?" Claude asked.

She took a steadying gulp of air. "Our place; the pharmacy was ransacked. Nancy... Nancy is hurt real bad. Sam is working on her now. You've got to come." Ellen left without waiting for a response and ran back to the new hospital.

"How is she, Sam?" Claude asked quietly, not wanting to disturb the other patients.

"Too early to tell." Sam sat heavily in the office chair. "Whoever did this came in real quiet. We were upstairs and never heard them. They knew exactly what they were looking for and where to go. Nancy's room is downstairs. Claude, she was tied, gagged, and beaten. My medical opinion is she was punched hard enough to knock her unconscious, then gagged and tied. The beating was brutal and it was very methodical."

"What's missing?"

"Heavy drugs: codeine, morphine, methadone, valium, lunesta. I haven't taken a full inventory, but those were obviously what they were after. It's likely they didn't know what Restoril, Librium, Naltrexone, Ativan, Klonopin, Tranxene, or Fioricet are, or those would be missing too. At a cursory glance, the synthetic morphines weren't touched either."

"Did any of the patients hear anything?" Claude asked.

"I don't think so. You can talk to them if you think it will help." Sam stood without another word and walked back into the new surgery to check on Nancy.

"Hello, Mr. Polez, do you remember me?" Claude said. Kyle was sitting up in bed, trying to eat his oatmeal left handed.

"Yes, I remember you. You're the sheriff, the one who found me, right?"

"That's right. Did you hear anything last night, Kyle? Anything at all?" Claude started his interrogation with easy, non-threatening questions.

"I heard the front door open and close. Then footsteps and another door open. That's about it, Sheriff. I drifted away after I heard the second door. Nurse Nancy gave me a shot about ten minutes earlier and I was starting to fade in and out," Kyle answered.

"Do you know what time that was?"

"I haven't a clue; my watch doesn't work anymore."

"Did you hear any voices?"

"No, I didn't. Sorry."

"Thanks for answering my questions, Kyle." Claude started to leave and stopped. "Have you remembered anything about your past yet?"

"No, it's very frustrating to me."

After the sheriff left his cubicle, Kyle rested his head against the pillow and stared at his bandaged hands.

Oh, you'd be surprised at what I'm remembering, Sheriff.

Claude parted the curtain around the prisoner and stepped closer, noting the blood soaked sheets and the efficiently sharp scalpel lying on the top sheet near the foot of the bed. He felt for a nonexistent wrist pulse, and backed out.

"Dr. Cory, can I see you for a minute?" Claude said outside the door to the new surgery.

"You can add murder to the robbery charges. We lost Nancy," Sam said. Even his hardened medical demeanor couldn't hide the sadness in his voice.

"Make that a double murder. My prisoner has had his throat slit. Would you confirm death for me please?"

The two stood within the curtained area, while Dr. Cory confirmed death.

"I'm going to estimate the time of death to be approximately six hours ago. Cause of death is a severed carotid artery, and the weapon is right there, one of my own scalpels."

"Does this appear to you to be the same MO as the other murders?" Claude asked, wrapping the scalpel in a towel.

"I couldn't say if the murderer was known to the prisoner since we kept him sedated, however the sliced throat and leaving the locally acquired weapon in plain sight sure smacks of the same killer."

Claude ran his fingers through his thinning hair. "This last murder was pretty brazen. There are, what, six other people in the building? All of the other attacks were in private homes of single people. I'm wondering if this was a copycat murder."

"I don't know, Claude. Without communications not that many know about the killings or the details. So if it is a copycat, it would be another close local."

"Now that's even more disturbing. Two killers on the loose."

Kyle closed his eyes, feigning sleep, and concentrated listening to the talk on the other side of the curtain, wondering how he could use this information.

CHAPTER THIRTY-TWO

"By my calculations, tomorrow is February first, right?" Adele asked the group over their usual soup for lunch.

"Yes," Chet answered. "I've been keeping careful track so I can plan holiday meals for us."

"That's sweet, Chet, though it brings to mind something else. Has anyone else noticed how warm it is?"

"I wasn't going to say anything to jinx us," Jeff said. "This is unusually warm for this time of year. I'm not going to complain though, and I'm hoping it means an early spring. I couldn't have asked for better company to be isolated with." He gave Adele's knee a squeeze under the table. "I love all of you, but I'm ready to get out of here, even if it's only for a walk in the woods!"

"Did you hear that?" Chet asked. The three of them, Chet, Adele, and Jeff, decided to take a snowshoe walk around the resort to get some fresh air and to give Aaron and Beth some alone time. The low rumble sounded again.

"Jeff?" Adele said in alarm. The last time she heard something similar was right before the avalanche weeks ago.

He instantly understood what was concerning her. "It's got a different sound to it and there isn't the telltale ground vibration, so I'm pretty sure it isn't another avalanche. Just listen." They all stood still, eyes closed.

Adele laughed. "It's thunder!" She turned in a circle and pointed to the dark clouds in the distance.

"Rain will certainly beat down some of the snow, that's for sure," Chet responded.

"We don't want the snow to melt *too* fast; that could cause flooding, right?" Adele asked.

"Yes and no. We are at such a good pitch on the mountain that any flooding would be minimal. That being said, the storm drains hold only so much. Combining snow melt and rain could overwhelm even the best system," Jeff told him. "I'm not going to worry about it." He took a deep lung full of clean mountain air and slowly let it out. "It's got to be close to seventy degrees." He smiled broadly. "Come on, let's take a look at the road where the avalanche snowpack is."

The trio wandered around the compound for an hour enjoying the warmth from the high sun while inspecting various areas they hadn't seen for two months.

"Oh my, look!" Adele gasped and pointed. She had faced toward the office and spotted the tops of several domes that were previously buried.

"This lightens my heart," Chet said solemnly. He took a deep breath, and with tears running down his cheeks, said, "I miss Matthew. Maybe soon we can put him to rest."

The next rumble of thunder was much louder, and the now hazy blue sky took on a bruised look. The deep purple and black clouds moved in quickly.

"I think it's a good time to head back," Jeff said, patting Chet on the shoulder. They slogged through the slushy snow and arrived at the dome as the first drops of rain came down. Setting the three pairs of snowshoes tail down into the snow so Aaron and Beth could see they had all returned safely, they hurried under the carport to watch the rain.

"Never thought I would enjoy rain so much," Adele sighed. She opened the unlocked door to her immobile car. Under the seat she found her umbrella and in the glove box was a couple of new, cheap rain ponchos.

"Why do you have more than one poncho, Adele?" Chet asked.

"Um, well, I consider them emergency supplies and therefore disposable. Now I guess nothing is disposable." She handed Jeff and Chet a poncho and opened her umbrella. The wet onslaught still caused her to hurry to the dome.

Moments later they saw Aaron and Beth making a mad dash for them and were ready to open the door to let them in. A loud thunderclap sounded as they stumbled inside.

"Geesh, that came up fast," Aaron said, accepting the towel Adele handed him. Another roar of thunder and a simultaneous lightning bolt followed. All eyes were focused on the dramatic change occurring on the other side of the triple paned window.

"Oh, crap," Aaron said quietly, "I just thought of something. The windmills aren't grounded now that they are disconnected from the generator. They could easily get hit and that would direct the charge to the battery wiring and to the inverter. I've got to get over there and disconnect everything. Run some water if you need it!"

Adele grabbed her big flashlight and handed it to him. Jeff tossed him one of the new packs containing a poncho. Chet put his poncho back on and the two headed into the storm.

Inside the power dome, Aaron began flipping switches while Chet held the light steady. Another roll of thunder shook the building slightly. "I sure am glad these domes are as sturdy as they are."

"Are we in any danger of fires?" Chet asked, holding the light while Aaron opened the door to the feed box of the three windmills. He pulled a breaker to the off position.

"Not anymore," Aaron said in relief. "While we're here, though, I think we should check the units, office, and the kitchen... just in case."

The two men took either side of the hotel hallway and scouted, mostly by smell, for any electrical fire. The snow melting away from the windows, adding hazy daylight, helped to speed the process as they made their way to the main building.

Nearing the dining hall, Chet spotted something huddled on the floor and soundlessly raised his fist in a signal for Aaron to stop. He inched forward, and then knelt down.

"Well, hello there, girl." Chet cautiously stretched his hand out. The dog growled faintly. "That's okay, you're a good girl." The dog lowered her head and whimpered. Chet gently pet her head and ran his hand down her side. "Aaron, can you get a bowl of water and anything for her to eat, even a cracker." Aaron slipped past them and into the dining hall. He returned a few minutes later with the water.

"I couldn't find anything edible. Is she hurt?"

"I don't think so. What I'm pretty sure of is she's starving and in labor." Chet slid his hand under the dog's head and lifted, so she could drink. "See what you can find for us to make a stretcher. She needs food and warmth or she and the puppies will die."

Aaron fashioned a large sling out of a sheet and lined it with a bath towel. Together they lifted the ailing dog onto the towel and Aaron tied it to Chet. Chet pulled the poncho down, covering the dog, protecting her from the rain.

"Everything okay?" Jeff asked when the two arrived back at the smaller dome where the other three waited. He raised his brows in question when he saw the bulk under Chet's raincoat.

"We found another survivor," Aaron said, helping to remove the poncho and then holding the weight while Chet slipped the sling off. He carried his package closer to the woodstove and opened the sheet.

"A dog!" Adele exclaimed joyfully and knelt beside her. "What's wrong with her, Chet?" she asked when the dog was unresponsive to the petting.

"I think she's half-starved *and* she's in labor." He placed his big hand gently on her belly and felt another contraction. "Is there any rice left over from last night? Or pasta?"

Adele got to her feet and checked the silent refrigerator to find it nearly empty. She pulled a can of chicken noodle soup and a package of noodles out of the cupboard and quickly fired up the camp stove to cook the pasta.

Chet took the bowl from Adele and let the dog smell it. She struggled to half sit and gulped the food down and took more water. Her head dropped to the floor, exhausted, and her tail thumped a couple of times in appreciation before she fell asleep.

"How did she get into the dome?" Jeff asked, watching the golden retriever sleep. "And what are you going to call her?"

"I think Lucky would be an appropriate name," Chet said, stroking the dog's silky head with a wet towel to loosen some of the caked on mud and ice. "Or maybe Stormy. I like Stormy." He continued to wash the dog. "I hate it when people let their pets loose to fend for themselves. I know these are desperate times, but it still isn't right."

"Aaron, can you give me a report on the power status?" Jeff said, changing the subject from Chet's justified ire.

"Everything is shut down until this storm passes. I think we caught it in time. We checked each room for any electrical fires and didn't find any, although we stopped looking when we found Stormy. I think we should go over things again tomorrow during the daylight," Aaron said, glancing out the window at the deepening gloom.

Adele and Beth lit the two kerosene lamps and placed them on the tables. Then Adele lit the large propane lantern and set it near Chet. It seemed dark inside. They had all gotten used to electric lights again quickly.

"How long do you think it will be before she starts having the puppies, Chet?" Beth asked.

"I don't know," he replied. Stormy let out a groan and another whimper and began panting. The first puppy made his appearance.

Adele pulled Jeff off to the side. "I think we should have dinner here. I can whip up some chicken chili that should satisfy everyone and that way there is no pressure on anyone, especially Chet."

"Good idea. We won't ask, just go ahead and make it. I'll pour the wine. By the way, what kind of wine goes with chili?"

"Beer," she replied with a smirk.

Adele left a pillow and two blankets on the couch for Chet, though she wondered how much sleep he would get. There were now two adorable puppies and Stormy wasn't done.

Beth burst through the door while it was still pre-dawn. "How many?" she asked excitedly, kneeling next to the mound of towels that covered the new family.

Chet yawned. "Three pups, two male, one female, and one stillborn. I think she's done." He reached over and stroked Stormy's head. The new mother wagged her tail slightly and licked Chet's hand. She nosed one of the pups back into the group when he wobbled away blindly.

Adele and Jeff emerged from their bedroom, roused by the arrival of Beth. "It's been an exciting night," Jeff said sleepily. Adele moved to the kitchen and started heating water for coffee, something they were all going to need.

"I tried to keep her at home, honestly," Aaron said, following his wife. "She was too anxious to see the babies. I think it has her clock ticking." He gave Beth a hug.

"I put some extra water on to heat, Chet, in case you want me to make rice for Stormy," Adele said. "What can we mix with it?"

Chet stood and stretched. By the looks of the blankets, he had slept on the floor. "Thanks, Adele. The rice is good, and I'm sure she would eat it plain, although a cup of water with a bouillon cube will make it better and give her some fluids. I think she's so hungry she'll eat anything."

"Well, *Dad*, I think after coffee Aaron and I will go finish checking the domes. We need to find out how she got inside," Jeff said. "And by the looks of it, *you* need a nap. When we get back, we need to figure out the next step."

"Next step?" Adele queried.

"They can't stay here. There isn't any place for Chet to sleep except on the floor."

"I've been thinking about that, boss. Now that I'm not sharing my bedroom, I think that would be a good place for the pups and I can keep them corralled as they get bigger." Chet turned to Aaron. "I'll need some kind of box, a big box, for all of them to stay in for a couple of weeks. One with high enough sides to keep them confined when they get adventuresome."

"It doesn't matter, Jeff, it's part of *your* new rules." Adele pushed the hunting rifle into his hands. "None of us go anywhere alone, and none of us go out unarmed." She put her hands on her slender hips and blocked the doorway.

"She's right, boss-man. Take the rifle." Aaron slung the shotgun across his shoulder and Adele stepped aside. "Chet is really excited about the dogs," Aaron commented while he and Jeff slogged through the slushy snow.

"I noticed. It makes sense, if you think about it. You have Beth and I have Adele. He doesn't have anyone and a dog is a good substitute for him. Chet is a warmhearted, caring person, and now he's got four beings to shower with attention," Jeff replied.

"How long do you think it will take before he has them all named?"

Jeff laughed. "He probably has already done that and we don't know yet."

"I think I should put the power back on before we go wandering around in the dark," Aaron said.

"Good idea. It will make it much easier and quicker being able to see," Jeff agreed.

Inside the maintenance dome, Jeff held the flashlight while Aaron reconnected wires and began flipping switches.

"There, now we have lights in here, in the office building, both home domes, and we have water."

"That should make our ladies happy," Jeff said.

They approached the back of the hotel dome that they had been using for an entrance and found the window completely broken.

"Was this broken when you found the dog?" Jeff asked.

"I honestly don't remember. It could have broken like this if she forced her way in to get out of the storm. Although it would have been an easy entrance for a dog if it had already been broken out."

"But you're not sure?"

"No."

"Then make sure you have a round chambered. We go in quiet." Jeff led the way, silently thanking Adele for forcing him to take the rifle.

The rain had stopped overnight and the brilliant sunshine that graced the day filtered in through the various windows, illuminating their way along the hotel corridor. They stopped at the big glass doors that led into the dining room.

"Did either of you check out the kitchen or dining room?" Jeff whispered.

Aaron shook his head, and pushed firmly on the heavy doors. Once inside the gloom, they each took a side, allowing the sunlight from the corridor to lead the way into the empty room. Jeff stepped on something near the bar and glass crunched under his foot. Now on alert, they quietly made their way to the swinging door leading into the kitchen.

With each on either side of the door, Jeff risked a peek through the small window. The door burst outward sending Jeff against the wall. Aaron fired the shotgun at the fleeing figure. Aaron approached the person lying on the floor. He pushed the body over with his foot while maintaining a vigilant aim. Cal groaned.

Jeff came up behind him as two more men came charging into the room. They all froze.

"On your knees," Aaron said in his deepest, most menacing voice. The men held out their hands, and remained on their feet.

"Hey, we didn't know anyone was here," Enno said. "We only came looking for food."

"I said, on your knees," Aaron repeated and leveled the shotgun at the duo. Jeff kept a bead on the second, shorter man.

"Okay, okay," Enno said, bending over as if to comply. He pulled the long-bladed knife from his boot and lunged at Aaron. Aaron deflected the wicked blade but it still caught him in the thigh.

Derick raised his weapon and Jeff pulled the trigger on the hunting rifle, sending the shorter man flying backward in a bloody heap. He turned in time to see Enno go in for another jab, and pulled the trigger again.

"Are you okay?" Jeff asked Aaron, who had dropped to the floor.

"That son of a bitch stabbed me in the leg! Man, does that hurt!" Aaron looked up at Jeff. "Hey, you could've hit me!"

"Never, my friend, I'm too good of a shot. Let's get you into the hall where there's more light."

"Take care of this trash first."

Jeff checked Enno first, and, finding him dead, checked the one crumpled against the wall. The last was Cal, the young man that took the shotgun blast to his back. No one was left breathing. The menacing force was now leaderless.

Jeff helped Aaron into the hallway and propped him against the wall facing the offices. He handed him the shotgun and said, "Keep an eye out, there could be more." He wrapped a towel around Aaron's thigh.

"Would you rather I do that?" Chet asked, causing Jeff to jump.

"Geeze, man, you almost gave me a heart attack! How'd you get here so fast?"

"I was already outside when I heard the first shot, so I ran. I can be real quiet when I want to," he said calmly. "What happened?"

After Jeff and Aaron quickly explained the circumstances, Chet said, "Jeff, I think you and I should clear the rest of the building." He looked down at Aaron, checked the long gash, and adjusted the towel. "It's just a scratch. Don't go anywhere." He chuckled, and, following Jeff, they flipped on every light switch they came across.

They checked the arcade and the gym, then Jeff's office.

"How deep do you think we should go, Chet?" Jeff asked, deferring to the one with military experience.

"It *feels* like it was only those three. I could be wrong though. I'll be honest with you, boss, that knife wound isn't just a scratch. It looks deep and I think we should get Aaron back so I can tend to it."

"Let's listen for a one minute. If we don't hear anything we'll go."

Chet closed his eyes in concentration. Jeff was tempted to do the same but knew one of them needed to watch as well as listen. When the minute was over, they double timed it back to Aaron.

Beth hovered over Aaron while Chet cut away the pant leg. She groaned a sob when she saw the deep gash.

"This is going to take stitches," Chet announced. "I can't do anything with him on the couch like this, it's too low."

Jeff grabbed Beth by the shoulders and looked her in the eye. "Beth, go get two clean sheets and a blanket." He and Adele cleared the dining table of everything. With the blanket as a pad and a sheet to protect it, the men lifted Aaron onto the covered table and Chet went to work cleaning the wound.

"I thought you said he needed stitches," Jeff commented quietly.

"He does, only I don't have any sutures. A dozen butterflies will have to do, boss. I've put on some Neosporin, which is better than nothing, barely. I'm concerned, though. I doubt that knife was very clean." Chet expressed his fears in a whisper, allowing the running water to wash his hands to cover his words.

Another, milder storm moved in during the night.

"Hey, boss, we should do something about those bodies in the main complex. They're going to start smelling soon, if they haven't already."

"I'd forgotten completely about them. Maybe we should go *before* lunch. I don't want to lose some of your cooking," Jeff replied.

"No need, Jeff," Adele said slipping her arm into Jeff's. "Beth and I took care of it yesterday. We dumped the bodies where Tanner's was, which is gone now, by the way, and we collected two rifles and two knives. They're in the weapons closet."

Jeff and Chet stared at the announcement.

"You never cease to amaze me." Jeff kissed the top of her head.

CHAPTER THIRTY-THREE

"We have a problem, Jeff," Chet said quietly even though he had asked Jeff to join him outside. "Aaron is running a fever, and the wound is looking infected. One of us needs to go into Avon for antibiotics."

"During our evening walk last night, Adele and I noticed the snow is melting fast, real fast, even the avalanche slide. I think I can get the truck through what is left. That way it should take less than an hour to get there, provided nothing else is blocking the way. That also means we can be back tonight. First I need to put a battery back in the truck."

"I'll pack you some sandwiches," Chet said, hurrying back inside.

"I think that's a reasonable plan. When do we leave?" Adele asked when Jeff proposed the idea to her.

"I was thinking of taking Chet."

"Chet? He's our only medic and you know Beth won't leave Aaron's side. You're stuck with me since we've agreed *no* one goes anywhere alone," she insisted, crossing her arms over her chest.

"You're right. Dress warm, and don't forget your pistol and extra magazines, and I'll grab the lunch Chet is packing for us. We leave in fifteen minutes."

"Well, that wasn't so bad," Jeff said, coming to a stop on the other side of the drift.

"Not bad at all. We only got stuck twice with snow up to the axle. I'm glad you remembered to put a shovel in the truck," Adele said sarcastically. The quarter mile drive took them an hour, with Adele doing most of the shoveling and Jeff blasting through the deep spots only to get stuck again.

"It won't be as bad going back though, and from here out it should be much easier," Jeff said.

"Look over there, Jeff. There's smoke coming from the chimney and there's a bunch of snowmobiles parked there. Should we stop?"

"Another time maybe, right now we're on a mission. Aaron really needs those antibiotics."

They drove in silence until they reached the town limits.

"Without power, I wonder how the hospital has managed, or if they're even still open. I think we should stop in to the sheriff's office first." Jeff parked the old truck in front of the municipal building, not bothering to turn around.

"Jeff! Good to see you," Claude greeted him. "Who is this lovely lady?"

"Adele Michaels, meet Sheriff Claude Burns. Adele is, *was,* one of my long term guests. Claude, Aaron is really sick and needs antibiotics. Is the hospital open?"

"It's open, but we had to relocate it. It's only a short walk, come on," Claude said.

"I'd rather drive so we can leave right from there," Jeff pressed.

"I sure wish we had something like this truck. It would have made a number of things so much easier," Claude said.

"Tell you what: once Aaron is back on his feet, I'll have him start on fixing up the Willy's jeep for you," Jeff offered.

"Deal! Make a right here."

Claude led them into the new hospital to find Dr. Sam Cory sitting at the desk filling in a chart.

"Dr. Cory, nice to see you again." Jeff held out his hand. "I'm glad you're here. Aaron suffered a knife wound a couple of days ago and now it's infected."

"Is he running a fever?"

"Yes, Chet said it's 103°. He butterflied the gash after cleaning it, however, it still festered. Do you have some antibiotics?" Adele asked.

Kyle's eyes flashed open when he heard Adele's voice.

"Of course. I'll be right back."

"Oh, and doctor, do you have any sutures you can spare?"

He descended the basement stairs. A few minutes later he was back and closed and locked the door behind him.

"Why do you lock the door?" Jeff asked. "I thought this was a safe town."

"Since the EMP, it's not as safe as it once was," Claude said.

"We had a break in about two weeks ago," Sam told them. "Whoever it was took more than half of the painkiller drugs, killed one of my nurses, and then killed one of my patients."

"After looking around the next morning, I found snowmobile tracks leading up Hog Back. There was no way for me to follow except on foot," the sheriff continued. "Several days before that, we had another run-in with the guys on the sleds. It was a member of their gang that was here being treated for gunshot wounds that was killed, his throat slit. I think it was to keep him from talking. I kept the sled they left behind, but during the night, someone came by and took it. Nothing is safe anymore."

Jeff and Adele exchanged a glance. "On our way here we spotted a number of sleds parked at a house about two miles south of the resort," Jeff said. "The timetable would fit in with an incident we had too. Three guys broke into the office section of the domes. In defending ourselves, Aaron and I killed all three." Jeff looked at the sheriff when he made that confession. "It's how Aaron got stabbed. One of the guys, a kid, really, looked familiar. Maybe he was a local, but I don't know."

"This is getting interesting. There's a local family here, the Cummings, who has a teenaged son and a house up on Hog Back," Claude said.

"Wait a minute. Are you talking about Cal?" Sam asked.

"That's him, why?"

"Cal was in here asking for some aspirin; he saw me go downstairs."

"The pieces are falling into place," Claude said. "There were six in that snowmobile gang, adding Cal, and taking out the four dead, leaves a minimum of three left up there. That's a number I can handle. Let's talk outside, Jeff."

"Here is a kit I made up for Chet. I'm familiar with his background and that he knows how to use this," Dr. Cory said to Adele. "There are injectable antibiotics, plus syringes and a couple of Z-packs. I added some sutures of various sizes, and a few painkillers. By the time he runs out of these, the roads should be open."

"Thank you so much, doctor. I don't know what we would do without Aaron," Adele said.

"There is something you might be able to help us with," Dr. Sam said quickly. "Shortly after the EMP, Claude was up Hog Back and found a man half buried in the snow slide. Maybe you can identify him for us."

Adele's back went rigid and her eyes went wide with fear. "Where?" she barely whispered. Dr. Cory pointed to the closed curtain, concerned with her response. She took a step forward, the doctor at her side. He pulled the curtain aside.

"Good morning, Kyle," the doctor said.

"Good morning, Dr. Cory. Do I have a visitor?" Kyle kept his face neutral even though the rage was coursing through his veins at the sight of Adele. His hands twitched at the thought of placing them around her neck.

"Kyle doesn't remember anything before the avalanche. He had a wallet on him, so we know his name is Kyle Polez and he's from Texas. Do you know him, Adele?"

Adele looked at him, her heart beating so loudly she was sure they both could hear it. There had been a moment of recognition in Kyle's eyes and it was gone just as quickly.

"No, I don't. Sorry." She spotted his bandaged hands. "What happened to his hands?"

"Frostbite," the doctor said. "I'll be back later, Kyle."

Adele went straight for the door and once outside, leaned against the building, hyperventilating.

"Adele, what's wrong, honey?" Jeff grabbed her before she collapsed.

"It's Kyle," she sobbed into his chest.

"So you *do* know him?" Dr. Cory asked, confused. She nodded silently.

Jeff immediately went on alert. "He's alive?"

"What's going on?" Claude asked, looking bewildered.

"It seems that Adele knows our amnesia patient," Sam explained. "Why did you say you didn't?"

Adele pushed away from Jeff to face the sheriff and the doctor.

"Kyle Polez, master architect of the most secure websites in the world, is a sadist and very violent. He's also my ex-husband. I divorced him a year ago, after he broke several of my bones," Adele confessed with a suppressed whimper. "Last time I saw him he was in a secure mental hospital in Texas. That is, until he showed up at the domes right after the EMP."

"He also is the one who started the avalanche. He was trying to kill Adele when his shot went wild. He was swept away by the snow slide and we thought, hoped, he was dead." Jeff tightened his grip on the woman at his side.

The sheriff wiped his hand over his face in thought. "He tried to *kill* you? No wonder Henry didn't like him." He looked at the doctor.

"Can you discreetly keep him sedated until I decide what we should do?"

"Sure. His physical therapy is next, and I usually give him a pain pill afterward."

"What's the physical therapy for?" Jeff asked.

"Being buried in the snow for forty-eight hours cost him fingers and toes. He's still learning how to walk without the counterbalance of his toes," Dr. Sam explained.

"Please be extra cautious around him, doctor. He's a master manipulator and is very, very good at lying," Adele said, regaining some of her composure. "He's a dangerous man. Don't ever let your guard down around him."

"Now, Jeff, about this other matter," Claude brought him back to their previous conversation.

"Yes, Sheriff, we can wait while you round up a posse," Jeff said, which made the sheriff grin. "We can't stall too long, though. We must get this medicine back to Aaron; I can't lose him. Not only is he my best friend, he's also a genius. He even got our power up and running again."

"What?" both the doctor and the sheriff said in shock.

"When this is all over with, come up and see what he's done," Jeff offered.

Kyle smirked. His hearing was acute. So Adele's new boyfriend has power back on. Good to know.

CHAPTER THIRTY-FOUR

"We'll wait for you here, Sheriff," Jeff said, parking in front of the café. "Please don't be too long." He held Adele close, making small circles on her back. "The sheriff is a good man; he'll figure out what to do with Kyle. We get back to the dome and you'll be safe again."

"Will I? He found me once. He won't stop until I'm dead."

"I won't let that happen, I promise."

The sheriff knocked on the side window, causing them both to jump. He got in the passenger side and closed the heavy door.

"I've got three deputies and the mayor in back. Every one of them is a crack shot. I'll explain my plan on the way."

Jeff followed his own tracks up Hog Back Road through a light, misty rain. The old truck held steady to the pavement the melting snow exposed.

"The house where we saw the snowmobiles is a quarter mile up on the left," Jeff said to the sheriff.

"Stop here. Give us about ten minutes to get near the house, then drive on past. If they follow, they'll be boxed in between us. If they don't, we'll still take them by surprise. After you drop off Adele and the medications, come back for us. We will either need the extra gun or a ride home," the sheriff said, getting out of the truck.

Jeff took off, going a bit faster than he did coming down. When they got to the edge of the snow slide, he gave the old Chevy a bit more gas and plowed through his tracks only to get stuck halfway.

"Damn! We're stuck again. Adele, you take the medical kit to Chet, I'm going back to help the sheriff. When we're done there, his men can help me get out of this."

"But—"

"No buts, Adele, please, just do it. Save Aaron. Now go." He kissed her soundly and she got out, hiking the short distance back to the domes.

Jeff put the truck in reverse and backed up as far as he could, utilizing the downhill momentum and gravity to his advantage. When he finally cleared the drift, he turned around and drove back to the Cummings' house.

Adele trudged through the slushy snow, staying in the deep tracks left by the truck. She tucked the medical kit inside her jacket to allow both hands to be free to help keep her balance. When she spotted the office dome, she picked up her pace.

"Chet! Where are you?" Adele called out.

Beth stood from the couch where she had been resting near Aaron. "Chet's napping. I'll let him know you're back."

"Hi there, big guy," Adele said, smiling down at Aaron. "I've got the antibiotics for you. Chet will fix you right up. You'll be better in no time." Aaron smiled and drifted off again.

Chet looked through the kit Dr. Cory had put together. "This is terrific." He filled a syringe with antibiotics and injected it into Aaron's thigh. "Where's Jeff?"

"He went back down the road to help the sheriff. It seems the guys that broke in here were from a larger gang that's been causing a lot of problems, and that gang is housed only two miles from here," Adele said. "I'm going back."

"Adele, wait!" Chet grabbed her arm. "It's getting late. I'm sure Jeff would rather you wait here so he doesn't have to worry about you."

"I know you're right, Chet, but that doesn't stop *me* from worrying about *him*."

Chet laughed. "Welcome to the club. We *all* worry about him."

"With five of us, I think we can surround the house. Two in the back watching the rear in case they try to bolt; one on either side; I'll take the front. Don't let a baby face fool you, these are dangerous guys. They've committed several murders and raided the pharmacy of vital medicines. It's shoot to kill," Claude said.

"Claude…" Henry cautioned.

"Mayor, you're the leader, I'm the enforcer, and right now I'm also the judge and jury. This nest needs to be eradicated. Now go!" When Claude was sure everyone was in place, he called out.

"This is Sheriff Claude Burns. Everyone inside the house come out with your hands showing!" For the first few moments it was quiet, then there was the sound of glass breaking and a shot rang out, barely missing Claude. He dove for cover behind a fallen tree and returned fire.

Three of the remaining members of the now leaderless gang took up positions in the front of the house and fired heavily at the sheriff. The four younger members of Cal's gang, still high on drugs, tried escaping out the back, and were brought down quickly by the deputies waiting for them.

"You're surrounded! This is your last chance to come out," Claude called out.

The front door opened slowly. One man stepped out onto the once well kept porch, rifle in one hand, held out to the side. A second followed him in surrender. The unseen third man fired at Claude from behind the two others. Henry fired from the side, taking out the shooter, and Claude fired, taking down the two decoys. By prearrangement, the deputies rushed the back door to drive any others out the front.

"Sheriff, Marcus here! We've cleared the house. We're coming out."

The total was seven dead gang members, while the five law enforcement were unscathed.

"Good job, men! Let's drag this vermin to the edge of the woods."

"Sheriff!" Jeff called out coming up the driveway.

"Jeff, thanks for coming back."

"Sorry I couldn't make it back sooner, I got stuck in the drift. I sent Adele ahead on foot and should be getting back myself."

Looking around, Claude said, "I don't think we'll need a ride back after all. We'll just confiscate these sleds. They'll come in handy. Winter isn't over yet. There are six sleds here and only five of us.

Why don't you take one with you? That's a great truck, though I doubt it can get through everything."

They loaded the extra snowmobile into the back of Jeff's old pickup.

CHAPTER THIRTY-FIVE

"Allison? Are you home?"

"Hi, Mae. What can I do for you?" Allison said, opening the door.

"I saw the sheriff, the mayor, and a couple more men leave with Jeff in his pickup truck. I thought you might want some company until they get back." She smiled innocently. "I know I'm not real comfortable being alone, ever since my dad was..."

"Sure, come on in and have some tea with me. As much as I love both those men, there's still nothing like some girl talk," Allison said.

"You sit, let me refill the cups," Mae offered. "The teapot is in the kitchen?" She refilled the cups, took the pot back to the kitchen, and then stood behind Allison, a long filet knife in her hand. With one practiced move, Mae slit Allison's throat. She then dropped the knife in the sink and left by the back door.

The five lawmen happily drove the snowmobiles back into town, veering off to their own homes. Claude and Henry continued onward toward the house they shared with Allison.

"Honey, I'm home!" Claude called out. He looked at Henry and said, "I've always wanted to say that!" He let out a hearty laugh. He stepped into the dining room and saw Allison slumped over the table, one arm stretched out toward the overturned sugar bowl. "Allison...?" When he stood next to her and saw all the blood, his knees went weak and he went down.

Henry was quickly at his side and let out a sob when he saw. He pulled at Claude's arm, trying to get him to stand.

"She knew not to let anyone in!" Claude cried out.

"It has to be someone she knew well and wasn't threatened by," Henry said, wiping at his own tears. Through the blur he saw what her hand was pointing at. "Sheriff, pull yourself together and come here. Allison left you a clue."

In the spilled sugar was written MAE.

"Mae? Mae killed Allison? Why?" Claude slumped against the wall, unable to take his eyes off the spilled sugar.

"Why would she kill all those others?" Henry asked. "Think about it, Claude. Who is the least assuming person in town? Who is likely the most well known person? Who is the one person everyone would open their door for? And who would you least likely suspect? Mae. And you told me right from the beginning that a knife is a woman's weapon."

Claude pushed himself up, anger and hatred covering his grief. He pulled open the front door and ran out, Henry close on his heels. Long strides quickly put him at Mae's door. He didn't knock, he didn't call out. He kicked the door open and drew his pistol.

"Sheriff! How nice of you to visit me. Would you like some tea?" Insanity clouded her eyes.

"Why, Mae? *Why?*" he shouted at her.

"Why what, Sheriff?" she cocked her head to the side and looked past him to Henry, confused.

"Why did you kill all those people? Why did you have to kill Allison?" he choked out with a sob.

She looked back at him, her eyes clearing. "*Why NOT?*" she bellowed in anger and then laughed. "I take care of people all day long! I have for years! They share their ups and downs with me, but no one listens to me. I hear how happy everyone is. But I'm not happy, and if I'm not happy, no one can be happy and that includes you!" she screeched. Mae lunged at Claude with a knife she was hiding. He pulled the trigger and blew a large hole in her chest.

CHAPTER THIRTY-SIX

"How are you feeling, Aaron?" Jeff asked tentatively. He sat down in a chair next to the couch where his best friend had been resting. It had been three days since they had returned with the antibiotics.

"Like I was run over by a slow moving truck filled with monkeys," Aaron replied, trying to sit up straighter.

"Monkeys?"

"Well that's what I smell like, boss-man," he chuckled. "I can't wait to take a shower. Chet said I should be stable enough on my feet now. I'm only waiting for the water to heat. My wife even promised to wash my back." He waggled his dark eyebrows.

Jeff looked at Aaron with serious eyes. "Chet said it was touch-and-go for a while."

"Yeah, I know. The first injection didn't seem to do much and the second one about kicked my skinny butt. That Z-pack was the turning point. Makes me wonder where that damned knife had been.

Except I really don't want to think about that," Aaron said with a shudder. "I owe you one, Jeff. Thanks for risking going to town."

"You don't owe me anything. Just get better, or I'll start docking your pay," Jeff teased.

"And that woman of yours—I hear she walked the meds in over the snow slide."

"Yeah, she's really something…"

"We've been friends a long time Jeff, ever since we were kids. I can tell there's something on your mind," Aaron pointed out.

Jeff looked down at the floor, then up at the ceiling. Finally he looked back at Aaron and said, "I'm thinking of asking her to marry me."

Aaron's face split into a wide grin. "Go for it, Jeff," he said. "Marriage is a wonderful thing with the right person, and I think Adele is your right person."

"Can we talk to you, Sam?" Henry said, broaching a delicate matter.

"Of course." Dr. Cory eyed the two men he'd known for many years. "And Claude, I'm really sorry about Allison. She was a fine woman."

"Thanks. That's part of what I need to ask you about," Claude shuffled his feet. "Did you notice anything, anything at all about Mae that would explain why she did what she did?"

"No, but I will be the first to admit I was completely distracted by everything going on because of the EMP." Sam sat on the edge of his desk and ran his fingers through his thick dark hair. "I was losing patients daily. Some needed extended care or equipment that's no longer available, some couldn't get the medication they needed. In the last week alone, I've lost five children and seven adults from the lack of insulin."

"How many total have we lost, Sam?" Henry asked quietly.

"We lost a lot early on from lack of extended medications, several to suicide, and of course the fire. The total so far is a hundred and seventy-two," Dr. Cory answered, closing his eyes. "That's including the two we found at Taylor Mayde's station, all the thugs, and the ones Mae murdered." He paused. "I had been treating Mae for depression since the summer. I knew she was having a difficult time adjusting to her father's dementia and the demands it put on her, but I never would have guessed her to be homicidal, just sad."

"I have a theory now taking her depression into account," Claude said, "so hear me out. If she wanted a way to rid herself of her father and have it blamed on someone else, or at the very least not on *her*, then maybe the EMP gave her the means. By killing others who lived alone, and having someone else discover them, then she could kill her father and it would be blamed on this unknown killer. She would be rid of him and she would get off scot free."

"Why go after Allison then?" Henry asked. "Her father was gone and she was in the clear."

"I think I can answer that," Dr. Cory said. "Certain types of depression are a mask for more that's going on inside the brain. I think Mae's brain started to malfunction and part of her started to… enjoy the killing. She couldn't stop."

"Well, she's stopped now, and don't ask me to feel sorry for her." Claude stepped out into the unusually warm February air so the others wouldn't see his tears. Losing his wife was hard. For some reason, losing Allison was harder. A big piece of him was gone.

"Claude, with everything else going on, I forgot to mention that our Mr. Polez is missing," Dr. Cory said when he and Henry joined the sheriff on the front porch.

"What do you mean, missing?"

"I came downstairs this morning for his physical therapy and he was gone. He's been doing well with walking and keeping his balance, so it's possible he's only out taking a walk with this nice weather. He can't get far. He's doing well, not great, and fatigues easily."

"I thought you were going to keep him more sedated," Henry said, alarmed by the news.

"I have been. He's not a prisoner though. Henry, do you think Ms. Michaels is in danger?" the doctor asked.

"That depends on whether or not his amnesia is real."

Kyle had found his clothes in a box under the bed. With a couple of toes missing the boots were a bit loose, so he stuffed a torn up washcloth inside to keep them from tripping him up. The floppy fingertips of the gloves unnerved him and fueled his anger.

Before the doctor came for his therapy, Kyle dressed, put two bottles of water in his jacket pockets, and slipped out the front door.

He caught on quickly that the doctor was giving him more medication, not the same in smaller doses as he'd professed. It was easy enough to spit out the pills when the doctor wasn't looking. Kyle wanted a clear head for what he needed to do.

He strolled casually down the street, noticing no one paid any attention to him. This pleased him. He limped down the alleyway behind the Wilderness Outfitters. After breaking a window to get in, he filled a backpack with beef jerky and granola bars that had been overlooked, plus a sweater in case his jacket wasn't enough. This time he wasn't going to get caught short if he got cold. Kyle took a hat with earflaps and a pair of sunglasses, then searched for a weapon. A small, short bladed pocket knife was all he found and he shoved it in his pocket. Although he felt entitled to all the items he took, he wasn't a thief. He removed two one hundred dollar bills from his wallet and laid them on the counter.

Kyle began his slow, painful walk back up to the domes.

CHAPTER THIRTY-SEVEN

"Chet, I want to do some cooking, a joint effort between the two of us," Adele said over a cup of coffee. Jeff, Aaron, and Beth were at the dome office, deeply involved with something secret. "What kind of supplies do we have left?"

"I thought you would never ask!" Chet rubbed his hands together in delight. As he listed what they had, Adele listened intently, figuring in what she still had in the cupboards. "Jeff said you are a great cook. What do you have in mind?"

"If you will make up a tomato pasta sauce, I'll do a chicken stuffed manicotti," she announced after some thought. "All I need is bread crumbs and those dehydrated shallots."

"That's it?"

"Sometimes a simple dish can be magnificent. What got me thinking was finding a box of manicotti in the back of a cupboard," Adele told him. "I had bought a case of canned chicken for putting on salads, however, I didn't use many before the EMP hit and you were fixing all the fresh or perishable stuff first. For the topping, I've only got a small piece of cheese left though. We can do without."

"Will some pre-grated parmesan help?" Chet offered. Adele smiled.

They collected all the supplies needed and set to work in Adele's dome. Soon, mouthwatering aromas were emanating from her kitchen.

With far less snow to wade through, Kyle made it to the Geo Dome Resort in five hours. His feet and toes throbbed relentlessly from the long walk. Try as he may to ignore the pain, once he made it to resort, he had to rest or he knew he wouldn't have the strength to do what he had to do. The hatred and anger boiled up in him and consumed his thoughts. She had to die and so did that new boyfriend of hers. Without snow on the hillside roads now, there weren't any footprints to give away that he was there or where he went. Hiding in the back seat of a now derelict car, he took one half of a pain pill and slept.

Chet added another pinch of spice to his tomato sauce bubbling gently on the edge of the woodstove. Adele dipped a clean spoon into the sauce and tasted, letting out an appreciative moan.

"That's almost too good to put on my meager contribution," she said, smiling at Chet.

"Meager? Not even close. If you ever need a job as an assistant chef, let me know. I'd hire you in a heartbeat." Their banter was the easy conversation of friends as Adele set her filled casserole dish on the woodstove trivet, and covered it to help keep the heat in.

"How are Stormy and the puppies doing?" Adele asked, changing the subject. She knew she was a good cook, but she still felt inadequate next to Chet and the compliment embarrassed her.

Chet laughed, delighted to talk about his dogs. "Stormy is finally gaining some weight back, and the puppies are growing daily. They are climbing all over the place. You want one?"

"Ah, no, not yet. Have you named them?" Adele asked.

"Of course I have. The female is Pearl and the two males are Buster and Billy."

"I think it's time to set the table," Adele mentioned. "I can see Jeff coming across the yard. They must be done with whatever it was that was they were doing."

"On that note, I'm going next door to pick out some appropriate wine and change clothes. I'll be back in about twenty minutes." He stopped at the door and turned back to her. "Adele, this has been the most fun I've had in months." He gave her a warm, one-armed hug and hurried to the dome next door, waving a greeting to Jeff.

Although refreshed from his nap, Kyle still stumbled on swollen feet, making his way to the carport of the dome where he knew Adele was hiding out. He pulled the small knife from his inside pocket and opened the blade, placing it in an outer pocket as he watched Jeff approach.

With Jeff facing away from him, Kyle picked up a large rock, one that lined the walking path, and bashed Jeff in the back of the head.

Adele had seen Jeff nearing the house and waited to open the door for him. After a few moments, she opened the door to see Jeff on the ground and Kyle leaning over him with a large rock raised to strike.

"NO!" she shouted and sprinted out the door, slamming into Kyle, knocking him aside. The rock fell from his hands before he could again strike the prone figure on the ground.

Kyle roared and easily fought off Adele's attempts to disable him. He gave her a shove and quickly stood, grabbing her by the throat, forcing her to stand.

"Oh, how absolutely perfect," Kyle sneered at her, holding her with one hand. He balled his other hand into a fist and punched her, hard, not loosening his grip on her throat. Now, with both hands closing around her neck, he increased the pressure, blocking the flow of blood and oxygen to her brain.

She continued to struggle, though it was with diminishing effort. Adele began to see white spots blossoming behind her eyes and she went limp.

Kyle flung her motionless body to the ground and pulled the knife from his pocket. Poised over the two bodies lying still before him, he laughed in his madness and straddled Adele to finish her off.

Chet growled in outrage and grabbed hold of Kyle's short hair from behind and jerked him to his feet, preventing him from doing any more harm. He flailed helplessly in the big man's grip. Chet wrapped one arm around Kyle's neck and with the other, snapped his neck, and then dropped him like a deflated garbage bag.

Chet bent over Adele to feel for a pulse. She coughed and he turned her on her side. Assured she would be okay, he checked Jeff. The bruised and bloody lump on the back of his head was very obvious. Chet gently turned him onto his back to check his breathing and for a pulse.

Adele crawled over to Jeff on her hands and knees, laid her head on his chest, and sobbed.

Jeff moaned and his eyes fluttered open.

"You're sure?" Adele asked Chet, holding a snow filled baggie to her neck. The vivid purple bruises were already beginning to show, and the short finger marks were all too obvious.

"Chet broke his neck, Adele. That piece of shit won't bother you ever again." Aaron looked at Chet. "Remind me never to piss you off, big guy."

"I guess I got carried away. I only meant to pull him off you," he apologized to Adele.

"Well, I for one am glad you did what you did, Chet," Jeff said, pressing the ice pack to the back of his head. "We should probably take his body into town and let the sheriff decide what to do with it."

CHAPTER THIRTY-EIGHT

"It was self-defense, Sheriff. This guy was going to kill Jeff and Adele," Aaron explained to Claude.

"Why didn't they come in with you?"

"Neither one is in any condition to travel, even a short distance. Jeff has a severe concussion and Adele's throat is so bruised she can barely swallow. Chet is keeping an eye on them," Beth said.

"If you don't mind, I'd like to go back with you and check them over," Dr. Cory said. He stood and began restocking his black bag.

"And I'd like to question them," Claude added. "With the road now open, it shouldn't take long."

"Those are some nasty bruises, Ms. Michaels," Dr. Cory observed. He placed his hands gently on either side of her neck, the heels of his hands touching. "Swallow. Again." He flashed his penlight in her eyes. "I can't feel any damage beyond swelling. You were extremely lucky Chet showed up when he did."

Adele shuddered. "Yes, I know."

Dr. Cory bandaged the laceration on Jeff's head and flashed the light in his eyes, too. "Pupils are still a bit off, however, I think you'll be fine. You need to stay off your feet, don't move around too fast, and rest for the next few days. I'd like to see both of you at my office in a week."

Claude took their statements and stood to leave. He looked around and his attention caught on the overhead lights. "After three months without power, lights seem... odd. Like a miracle."

CHAPTER THIRTY-NINE

Claude and Henry sat in front of the town offices enjoying the warm spring temperatures.

"Late March has always been my favorite time of the year," Claude remarked. "The snow melts quickly, the grass is starting to turn green, trees are budding, and flowers are starting to bloom." A rumble in the distance made them both sit up straight, trying to figure out where the sound was coming from and what it was.

A convoy of military trucks and Humvees approached from the south and stopped in front of them. Two soldiers emerged from the hummer, one carrying an M-4 rifle.

"Good afternoon, Lieutenant. I'm Sheriff Claude Burns and this is the Mayor, Henry Hawkins," Claude said, noting the bars on the officer's collar. "What can we do for you?"

"Sheriff, Mr. Mayor, I'm Lt. Charles Manos. I'm here to relieve you of any responsibility for this town."

"Excuse me?"

"The entire country is under martial law, and it's now my job to take survivors to a relocation center further south. I'm hoping for your cooperation," Lt. Manos stated.

"I'm well aware of there being martial law; I instituted it myself right after the EMP. Rest assured, Lt. Manos, you will have our cooperation, even assistance, for the relocation of those who *wish* to go with you," Sheriff Burns stated.

"As for those who desire to stay, they will have our support in that too," Henry added.

"I see."

"I hope you do, Lieutenant. This may be a small town, but it's also a very self-reliant town filled with independent people. Some may not take well to being forced to leave," Claude said.

Lt. Manos studied the two men in front of him. "How soon can you organize a meeting where we can... discuss the situation with the citizens?"

"We should be able to spread the word by late this afternoon. Without lights we try to get everything done by nightfall, so everyone can get home safely," Henry said.

"Since you are familiar with martial law, sheriff, I'm assuming you've confiscated all firearms?" Lt. Manos addressed Claude.

"Oh, I'm quite familiar, sir. However, I elected to not do that. You must understand this small town is in the wilderness. We are isolated and vulnerable. Those here that have firearms are responsible *and* are our hunters. They've kept the town fed, and safe from predators, four-legged and two-legged."

He let the implication hang in the air.

"Perhaps that was your only option at the time. I understand. Is there someplace my troops can set up a bivouac?"

"The school yard has the largest open area. You're more than welcome to stay there. Please understand, we can't feed you," Henry said.

"Not a problem. We came with our own supplies."

Mike Miller guided his horses toward town, though for as many trips as they've made, he was sure the horses knew the way without him. He yanked hard on the reins, abruptly stopping the team, and waited for the military convoy pass by on the main road a half mile ahead. Trucks and horses didn't mix well, he knew, and didn't want this pair to get spooked and possibly injured. After the last vehicle went by, he proceeded with caution, staying off the main road and approaching the town from a back road.

Mike left his horses and wagon on a side street and let himself into the township office building.

"Mr. Mayor, what's the military doing here?" he asked, getting right to the point.

"Have a seat, Mike, we may need you again," Henry said. "The military is here to take people to a relocation center, to be taken care of they say. Not everyone will want to go."

"I get the impression from the lieutenant in charge that they may force the issue," Claude said. "I think you should take your horses and some supplies and stay at the dome until this is settled... one way or another. None of us want anything to happen to those horses."

Back at his farm, Mike emptied half of the firewood from the wagon and then filled it with as much hay and feed as would fit, and took a circuitous route up to the domes.

"Mike, what a pleasant surprise," Jeff greeted their guest. He ran his hands across the soft noses of the two horses. "What can we do for you?"

"There's a problem in town and I need sanctuary for the horses."

"What is it?"

"Military is in town. Sheriff Burns suggested I bring the horses up here to be safe."

"Military? Of course we'll house your horses. What kind of shelter do they need?" Jeff responded, wondering what the military was doing there. They settled on one of the empty carports further up the road and between the four men, unloaded the hay and straw quickly.

"What's the wood for?" Jeff asked when the firewood was exposed.

"I thought it might help pay for my stay," Mike answered.

"It's appreciated, but you know we would have taken you in regardless." Jeff thought a minute before going on. "Fortunately this unit has a woodstove so we can unload the wood here for you to use. Then we need to talk."

"Sheriff Burns said the military had come to take people to a shelter whether they wanted to go or not," Mike explained over a cup of tea. "I think he fears it's going to get messy when they try forcing the issue."

"Let's hope it doesn't come to that."

"Quiet down, everyone!" Mayor Hawkins pounded the gavel on the podium. The word spread fast that the army was in town and nearly everyone was there in the school auditorium for the meeting. Once order was restored, the mayor continued. "This is Lt. Charles Manos, who is in charge of the military side of this operation."

The lieutenant slid a glance at the mayor for his choice of words, and instantly knew what he was up against.

"Good afternoon. I'll make this as short of a meeting as possible so everyone can get back to their homes before dark. I've been assigned to offer transportation to everyone in need, to relocate to a shelter in Arizona, where the weather conditions are much more stable than here. You will be given shelter, food, medical care if needed, and eventually moved to permanent housing. The government has reestablished in Texas where the speaker of the house was on holiday with her family. Washington D.C. is now a hot zone."

"What do you mean, 'a hot zone?'" someone asked from deep within the crowd.

"There were three missiles launched at the United States on Thanksgiving, each one armed with a nuclear warhead. Two of those missiles detonated at a high altitude, wiping out the grid and all electro-nics. The third missile's target was the White House, and was followed by three more nukes. The entire East Coast is hot with radioactivity."

The news stunned everyone and the room went very quiet.

"How is it your trucks work and ours don't?" the same voice asked.

"The military vehicles are hardened against such threats," Lt. Manos explained. "It's going to be a long time before any infrastructure is operating, if ever." More stunned silence swept over the people. "Are there any questions before I continue?"

"Is there power at these relocation centers?" Claude asked.

"Yes. It isn't just vehicles that are hardened, Sheriff. Military posts everywhere have generators capable of providing power for all their needs. And before anyone asks, no, we can't just bring you one. Any other questions?"

"When can we leave?" Gwen Swanson asked. "I'm so tired of being cold."

"Thank you for asking, ma'am. This is a quick operation. We plan on leaving at noon the day after tomorrow. Everyone who wishes to relocate needs to pack, and pack lightly, and be here that morning for processing," Lt. Manos said. "And so there is no mistaking, there will be no second chances. We won't be back." He glanced over at the mayor and sheriff. "One more thing. For those who have firearms, I suggest you leave them with the sheriff. The country is under strict martial law and that means firearm possession in the relocation centers is cause for incarceration or execution."

Henry stood. "I'd like to address this meeting. I've been your mayor for twenty years. I know many of you personally, and I consider this town my home, and I'm staying. There are many of you who will be much better off going with the lieutenant, though. They can feed you, we can't. They can keep you sheltered and warm, we've struggled with that. They can protect you, and I know we've failed in that area, too. For everyone who wishes to leave, may God be with you." Henry sat down.

"Thank you, Lt. Manos. I wasn't sure you were going to give the people a choice," Claude said. They were still in the school, and a private had brought in hot meals and coffee for the four men that remained.

"People who want to relocate make for better citizens for us than those who are forced, sir," Sargent Kaplan explained, stirring real milk into his coffee. Manos and his assistant had discussed the issue before the meeting had even started. "We would rather have one willing person than ten reluctant."

"I hope you know what you're doing by staying, Mr. Mayor, Sheriff. It's going to be a hard life for you," Manos said.

The morning of the second day saw the school packed with people and suitcases. The vast majority of the population had elected to leave.

After the convoy left, Claude walked up to the dome to retrieve Mike and the horses.

"There are only a few people left in town, Jeff, everyone else went with the army. Do you have room for us up here?" Claude asked cautiously.

"Of course, sheriff. Who stayed?"

"Beside myself and Henry, there is Dr. Cory and his wife Ellen, Mike, of course, one of my deputies, Tighe Teagan and his wife and daughters, along with Janet Baler and Sherry Turner, two of the teachers from the middle school."

"How soon will you be coming back?" Jeff asked.

"Would this afternoon be alright? I think we all want to get out of town in case the military comes back."

"We'll get right on opening the other domes."

"Can we use your truck to move the hospital supplies? There's a lot."

Jeff tossed him the keys.

Lt. Manos returned to the town of Avon the day after the convoy left, with his driver and Sgt. Kaplan. Although he had said they wouldn't return, he felt compelled to give those who stayed behind one more chance. He found the town completely empty. It was as though a dozen people just vanished.

In the complete and total darkness, the electric glow from the domes shone like a beacon.

ABOUT THE AUTHOR

Deborah Moore is single and lives a quiet life in the Upper Peninsula of Michigan with her cat, Tufts. She was born and raised in Detroit, the kid of a cop, and moved to a small town to raise her two young sons, then moved to an even smaller town to pursue her dreams of being self-sufficient and to explore her love of writing.

KING ARTHUR AND THE KNIGHTS OF THE ROUND TABLE HAVE BEEN REBORN TO SAVE THE WORLD FROM THE CLUTCHES OF MORGANA WHILE SHE PROPELS OUR MODERN WORLD INTO THE MIDDLE AGES.

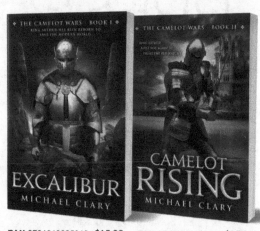

EAN 9781618685018 $15.99   EAN 9781682611562 $15.99

Morgana's first attack came in a red fog that wiped out all modern technology. The entire planet was pushed back into the middle ages. The world descended into chaos.

But hope is not yet lost— King Arthur, Merlin, and the Knights of the Round Table have been reborn.

PERMUTED
PRESS

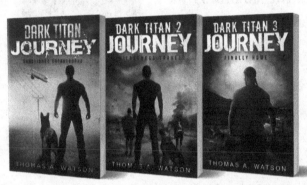

THE MORNINGSTAR STRAIN HAS BEEN LET LOOSE—IS THERE ANY WAY TO STOP IT?

An industrial accident unleashes some of the Morningstar Strain. The

EAN 9781618686497 $16.00

doctor who discovered the strain and her assistant will have to fight their way through Sprinters and Shamblers to save themselves, the vaccine, and the base. Then they discover that it wasn't an accident at all—somebody inside the facility did it on purpose. The war with the RSA and the infected is far from over.

This is the fourth book in Z.A. Recht's The Morningstar Strain series, written by Brad Munson.

PERMUTED
PRESS

GATHERED TOGETHER AT LAST, THREE TALES OF FANTASY CENTERING AROUND THE MYSTERIOUS CITY OF SHADOWS...ALSO KNOWN AS CHICAGO.

EAN 9781682612286 $9.99   EAN 9781618684639 $5.99   EAN 9781618684899 $5.99

From *The New York Times* and *USA Today* bestselling author Richard A. Knaak comes three tales from Chicago, the City of Shadows. Enter the world of the Grey–the creatures that live at the edge of our imagination and seek to be real. Follow the quest of a wizard seeking escape from the centuries-long haunting of a gargoyle. Behold the coming of the end of the world as the Dutchman arrives.

Enter the City of Shadows.

PERMUTED
PRESS

WE CAN'T GUARANTEE THIS GUIDE WILL SAVE YOUR LIFE. BUT WE CAN GUARANTEE IT WILL KEEP YOU SMILING WHILE THE LIVING DEAD ARE CHOWING DOWN ON YOU.

EAN 9781618686695 $9.99

This is the only tool you need to survive the zombie apocalypse.

OK, that's not really true. But when the SHTF, you're going to want a survival guide that's not just geared toward day-to-day survival. You'll need one that addresses the essential skills for true nourishment of the human spirit. Living through the end of the world isn't worth a damn unless you can enjoy yourself in any way you want. (Except, of course, for anything having to do with abuse. We could never condone such things. At least the publisher's lawyers say we can't.)